GRAVE JUSTICE

Other mysteries by Glen Ebisch:

The Crying Girl
A Rocky Road
Unwanted Inheritance

Avalon romances by Glen Ebisch:

To Breathe Again
Woven Hearts

GRAVE JUSTICE

•

Glen Ebisch

AVALON BOOKS
NEW YORK

Published by Thomas Bouregy & Co., Inc.
160 Madison Avenue, New York, NY 10016

Library of Congress Cataloging-in-Publication Data

Ebisch, Glen Albert, 1946–
   Grave justice / Glen Ebisch.
       p.   cm.
   ISBN 978-0-8034-9888-4 (acid-free paper)   1. New England—
Fiction.   I. Title.
   PS3605.B57G73   2008
   813'.6—dc22   2007037614

PRINTED IN THE UNITED STATES OF AMERICA
ON ACID-FREE PAPER
BY HADDON CRAFTSMEN, BLOOMSBURG, PENNSYLVANIA

Joseph A. Citro is the leading contemporary chronicler of supernatural and occult tales in the New England region. I have relied specifically on his account of Champ, the Monster of Lake Champlain as told in *Green Mountain: Ghosts, Ghouls, & Unsolved Mysteries* (Houghton Mifflin Company, Boston, 1994). For a more scientific and skeptical approach to these matters and for my brief discussion of "grave wax," I have consulted *Real-Life X-Files: Investigating the Paranormal* by Joe Nickell (University of Kentucky Press, 2001). I hope the tension between the desire to believe and the need to doubt gives the reader a balanced approach to these stories of the paranormal.

Chapter One

"Are you ready to talk to the dead?" Nicholas Krow asked.

Amanda Vickers smiled. Having just had a good meal and being comfortably ensconced in one of the two plush sofas that occupied the center of the elegant living room, she felt that even the chatty dead couldn't disturb her sense of well-being. Since the other dinner guests had momentarily disappeared to attend to various errands before the start of the séance, she felt at ease to banter with Nick.

"That depends on what the dead have to say. Or, let me rephrase that, what the medium *claims* they have to say."

"Don't tell me you're a skeptic?" Krow asked, raising an eyebrow in mock surprise. "You really shouldn't be, you know. You make your living by frightening people with stories of the supernatural, so isn't it a bit hypocritical of you to be a doubter?"

1

Amanda smiled again, not letting Nick's friendly jibes provoke her.

"I'm only an editor, Nick, not a writer. People send me stories about the supernatural, and they're printed in our magazine. I'm merely a conduit. I don't have to be a believer."

"However, you do have to admit that the "Weird Happenings" section goes a long way to keeping *Roaming New England* magazine profitable."

"But that wasn't our original intention," she replied, feeling a shade defensive about the magazine's use of the sensational. "Small magazines need a niche in order to survive; that's a fact of life in publishing. We started out playing the regional card, putting out a magazine about New England for people who live in the region or who once lived there."

"Or have some romantic notion of the area," Nick added with a wry grin. "Meaning that they haven't been through a New England winter in a long time."

"True enough. And that gave us a wide enough readership so we were getting along financially. Then we just happened to publish a story based on an old Vermont vampire legend, and suddenly we discovered a whole new market of people fascinated with the paranormal. So we piloted a column called "Weird Happenings." Our sales have doubled in the last year, and if the letters we get are any indication, it's largely because of that column."

"Which just goes to make my point," Nick said. "It's a sign of ingratitude to bite the ghostly hand that feeds you."

Amanda looked across the dimly lit room—its corners hidden in deep shadows—and wondered for an uncomfortable moment whether talking about spirits with such disrespect was really wise. Was it a way of tempting fate, like speaking of the devil? She quickly pushed her fears away as a silly case of nerves brought about by the upcoming séance, and turned back to Nick.

"What about yourself? We published one of your pieces. Do you believe?" Amanda asked, figuring that turnabout was fair play. After all Krow was an associate professor of psychology at the University of Maine in Portland who had made a hobby out of exploring the paranormal.

"I'm a scientist. I follow the evidence. As you'll recall, my article pointed out the lack of any proof of the supernatural in the so-called Bennington triangle. But show me a paranormal event that meets the criteria of scientific proof, and I'll shout it from the rooftops."

"So are you saying that you've never encountered a genuine paranormal event?"

"I've come across a lot of events that I couldn't explain, but just because I don't understand how something happened doesn't lead me to assume that it's paranormal."

"What more do you need?"

Nick stared down at the thick carpet, considering the question for moment.

"I'd need to have experts examine the evidence to make certain that there is no plausible natural explanation for the event. Then I'd need those same experts to show me some proof that supernatural causes brought it about."

"And none of these unexplained events you've experienced has been able to meet those criteria?"

"Sadly, no. The *possibility* of a supernatural explanation

is always exciting and fun when compared to a plain old, garden-variety factual one. But I've never come across a case where it was backed up by solid evidence."

"And you don't expect that tonight?"

"No, but it might have historical interest. You don't often get to see a good old-fashioned séance anymore."

"You mean there will be ghostly manifestations, ectoplasmic slime, and table rappings?" asked Amanda, recalling what she had read about nineteenth-century séances.

"As far as I know, even Anastasia Narapov doesn't go quite that far, but we will sit around a table with the lights dimmed, hold hands, and wait for her to contact her control or spirit guide."

"That would be Zaffir, the Persian prince from twenty-five hundred years ago that they were talking about at dinner," Amanda said.

"Right. And it should make for a good show. Most mediums today keep the lights on, ask you a lot of questions, then give you vague answers, which they refine based on your response. 'Cold reading,' it's called."

"Sounds like psychotherapy," Amanda said.

Nick laughed. "The two may be equally scientific."

They turned their attention to the round table at the far end of the room, as a thin, rather severe woman who had identified herself only as Mrs. Ames, the housekeeper began clearing it to get ready for the séance.

Amanda surveyed the room. With its heavy wine-colored draperies and mahogany moldings, it was probably meant to recapture the look of a Victorian sitting room and the atmosphere certainly seemed appropriately funereal for what was planned. In fact, Amanda thought the dark, rambling house could have been a stage set for a creepy movie. Located just a few blocks from the center of West Windham, Maine, a town about forty minutes northwest of Portland, the area was close enough to the Sebago Lake Region to get its share of tourists. As a result, many of the historic homes had been converted into bed-and-breakfasts or divided up for condominiums. This was one of the few large old houses to still be a private residence.

Amanda slipped off one of her tight pumps to stretch her foot out on the deep Persian rug. The shoes were a bit uncomfortable, but they went well with her dress. *A stylish appearance is important even at a séance,* Amanda told herself and smiled at her own weakness. "Control the things in life that you can control," her mentor in the newspaper business had once told her, and clothes were one of the few things that fell into that category. A good outfit made her feel as protected as a suit of armor.

"I'm getting a sense that we may both be a bit doubtful about the chances of talking to the spirit of Larissa Chastain tonight," Amanda said, as Mrs. Ames began arranging chairs around the table.

Krow nodded. "And it's unfortunate that we won't really be hearing from Larissa because I'm sure that what she has to say would be very interesting, especially to the police."

"You told me on the way out here that she was murdered during a robbery."

"I only got the basic facts from Will Chastain. She went shopping for the afternoon in Portland. While returning to her car, she was struck on the head and her purse was taken. There were no witnesses."

"If she had just finished shopping, it couldn't have been very late."

"Around five-thirty, I believe."

"This was about six months ago?"

"Exactly, as of today. That's why Martin picked tonight for the séance."

"And no one saw anything on a street in Portland at five-thirty in September? It wouldn't have been dark yet."

"Apparently she was cutting down a side alley to the parking lot when she was attacked. The police figure that the robber was waiting there for any likely victim, and it just happened to be Larissa's misfortune to come along."

Amanda slipped her other foot out of its shoe. She gave a small sigh of relief and wondered yet again whether it was silly to sacrifice comfort to fashion.

"What did you make of our host?" Krow asked, lowering his voice even though the room was empty except for Mrs. Ames, who was well out of earshot.

Amanda frowned, not certain what her opinion was. There had been only six people around the large dining room table for dinner: Martin Chastain; his son William; William's wife, Bethany; Eric Devlin, Martin's financial adviser; Krow; and herself. Normally she should have had plenty of opportunity to make a judgment about each of her fellow diners. But the conversation had remained polite, even reticent, giving her the odd feeling that she was in a well-scripted play where everyone was being careful to stay within the confines of their established roles.

She had suspected that the lack of spontaneity was largely due to an undercurrent of nervousness over the up-coming séance. Only Martin had talked about it openly and with excitement, at which time his family and Devlin had focused intently on their food, as if embarrassed, and said nothing.

"Hard to imagine Martin Chastain as a hard-driving multimillionaire businessman," Amanda finally answered. "He comes across as if he might be a colleague of yours."

Krow raised a quizzical eyebrow. "How's that?"

"The rumpled clothes, the somewhat vague way he has, as if he were thinking about more important things, his tendency to go into lecture mode like when he was talking about the séance. That all says college professor to me."

Krow tried to look offended. "Not all of us dress badly, are absent-minded, and dominate the conversation. But you are perceptive. Chastain started out as a teacher. He'd gotten his advanced degree in medical engineering from MIT and was teaching at some small college when he patented his first device."

"Some kind of medical micro-implant, you said earlier."

"That's right. Apparently he was on the cutting edge of developing those tiny machines that can be used to keep your heart going. Although I think that most recently, his company has been working on computerized artificial limbs. Anyway, after that first patent took off, he formed his own company and has never looked back. I suppose he's one of those rare people who's creative and also has a head for business."

"And his son, William, works for him?"

"Yes. I'm afraid that Will's always been a bit in his father's shadow. He went into engineering himself, but he's never had his father's creativity. Martin made him chief of engineering for the company, but I think Will has always felt that the position was a gift rather than something he'd earned. Although I doubt that it was much of a gift. From what Will tells me, his father rides all of his employees pretty hard, and his son most of all."

"And you know William well?"

"Pretty well. We were in the same class in college, and we both played soccer. When I got the job up in Portland, we renewed our friendship."

"So when his father decided to contact his dead wife, Will thought that your background qualified you as a knowledgeable, impartial witness, and he wanted you here as an observer."

"That's right."

"Why did he think one was necessary? Was he afraid that this medium would fleece his father out of a fortune?"

"That's part of it, I suppose." Nick said, frowning. "But it goes deeper. Larissa Chastain was Martin's second wife. His first wife, Will's mother, died some years ago, and Martin never showed any serious interest in women after that, until Larissa came along. She was thirty years younger than Martin, and he was instantly obsessed with her, according to Will. I think Will is afraid that his father is allowing his grief to carry him off the deep end. He wanted me here to serve as the voice of reason, just in case this medium brings back some really weird message from the beyond."

"Even weirder than 'give all your money to Anastasia Narapov'?"

"Maybe something like 'leave this life and join me in the next,'" Nick said softly.

"Would a medium say that?" Amanda asked, startled.

"The dead sometimes send strange messages."

She studied Nick's face to see if he was serious, but his expression was unreadable.

"If Larissa died six months ago, why didn't Martin try to contact her sooner?"

"This fascination with the next life only began after he met this Narapov woman. According to Will, he struck up a conversation with her at a social event in Boston two months ago. Apparently she has something of a reputation among the flaky affluent down there as a fortune-teller and mind reader."

"Why did he wait so long to schedule a séance?"

"From what I've heard she was rather reluctant to get involved, and Martin had a hard time talking her into it. She may have felt that contacting the dead takes a lot of effort, and then there's always the danger of accidentally opening yourself up to an evil spirit."

Amanda gave him a long look.

Krow spread his hands wide in front of him and grinned. "Hey, I'm just telling you what mediums say about this sort of thing."

"And why am I here? To back you up as the voice of reason?" asked Amanda.

"When you called to ask me what I knew about the Monster of Lake Opal, which was absolutely nothing, I figured that it was worth trying to get you to spend a day or two up here. I thought you might find this entertaining." He paused and gave her a lingering smile. "Almost as entertaining as I find your company."

Comments that might make her feel uncomfortable coming from another man, for some reason seemed like a natural, friendly give-and-take between the sexes when Nick said them. And Amanda had to admit that charming men were not so common as to be ignored. He was also smart, funny, and still looked athletic at thirty-five.

Amanda knew that he wouldn't go beyond flirting, unless given the appropriate signal. *Maybe someday,* she thought, *but not right now.* There was still the matter of Jeff to be settled. Avoiding that issue was the main reason she had agreed to make the trip up north from her office in southern Maine. She couldn't really justify it as a business trip because the Chastain séance was too current for the "Weird Happenings" column, which focused on paranormal folklore. Uncharacteristically, she was running away from a problem, and Nick had offered her an interesting place to hide.

"I find your company entertaining as well. And fortunately, tracking down the Monster of Lake Opal is Marcie's unpleasant job," Amanda said, referring to her assistant editor. "But if all went well today, she should have enough for that story by now."

"So you'll be going back tomorrow?" Krow asked, the disappointment in his voice not very well concealed.

"I have a magazine to put together. Deadlines wait for no woman," Amanda said, and decided to change the subject before Nick could come up with tempting reasons for her to delay her departure. "Why wasn't Narapov at dinner?"

"I gather she doesn't like to meet the other participants right before a séance. She'd probably say it confuses the lines of spirit power, but I'd guess she's just trying to avoid being accused of pumping people beforehand for information to use during the séance."

Amanda was about to ask another question when Martin

Chastain came into the room. In his middle sixties, he was tall and thin with a thick head of gray hair. He walked with his shoulders slightly forward, giving him a stooped, scholarly appearance, but Amanda had noticed at dinner that his pale blue eyes were piercing and alert. Next to him stood his son, in shape and size a younger, more vigorous version of himself. Bethany, William's wife, thin and birdlike, stood to one side glancing around the room anxiously, as if wondering whether the ghost had already arrived. Between the men was a short, rather plump woman with iron gray hair. She was wearing a bright red, woolen poncho over a rather drab dress with a full shirt.

"Our medium, I presume," Krow said, standing up and offering Amanda his arm as the others moved from the doorway in the direction of the table.

Amanda quickly forced her shoes back on and stood, being careful to smooth down her slim skirt.

"Ready to contact the other side?" he asked, with a mischievous smile.

"Sure," Amanda replied, trying to match his light tone.

But a sudden nervous fluttering in her stomach warned her that she wasn't being completely honest.

Chapter Two

Marcie wondered if she smelled like a wet sheep. Although she wasn't sure what a wet sheep smelled like, she figured that it couldn't be good. The thought came to her because she was wearing a heavy wool sweater and could feel the sweat running down her back in what she imagined to be raging spring torrents. *Why did I wear wool?* Marcie asked herself for the tenth time, even though she already knew the answer: she always wore a wool sweater in winter. She had three and rotated them through the workweek with a coordinated pair of corduroy slacks. It made getting ready for the day quick and easy, although she suspected at times that it lacked a bit in the style department. She had similarly matched cotton shirts and polyester slacks for spring and fall.

In addition to her sweating problem, her face was burning. Marcie wasn't sure whether it was windburn from the afternoon spent cruising around Lake Opal or the anxiety that arose from sitting across the table from a handsome man. She was tempted to cool herself down by dipping the end of a napkin in her water glass and patting her forehead, but she suspected doing that might seem a little odd in the middle of a restaurant. The Lonesome Pine wasn't the most elegant restaurant she'd ever been in, but bathing at the table was probably frowned upon. She glanced over her shoulder accusingly at the stone fireplace, where the dancing flames that were meant to provide warmth and coziness on a cool March night only served to worsen her situation.

"Are you okay?" Kirk Ames asked over the top of his menu.

"Sure," Marcie replied, and tried to sit up straighter in her chair. Good posture, someone had once told her, can make you look slimmer. With her sturdy figure, Marcie knew she needed every trick she could find. She still couldn't believe that he had asked her out. The question why kept resurfacing in her mind, no matter how many times she pushed it down.

"You look a little red in the face."

"I should have worn sunscreen. Who knew that the sun would be a problem during March in Maine?"

"It's all about the angle of the sun," Kirk said firmly, as if that explained everything one needed to know about the solar system.

"Right," Marcie said, unconsciously imitating her companion's laconic style.

Although they had gotten along fine out on the lake, the conversational ball had been dropped several times since they'd sat down to dinner. It didn't help that Kirk was the handsomest man she'd ever had dinner with. Just sitting across from him seemed to cause her tongue to grotesquely enlarge until she felt that even the simplest sentence would come out as babble. So she was reduced to saying virtually nothing. She almost wished that Amanda were there. Stylish, sophisticated Amanda would have no trouble keeping the conversation rolling along, but then, Marcie wondered, what chance would she ever have to capture Kirk's attention.

"And it didn't help that old Ben had boat problems. That kept us out there twice as long as necessary," Kirk added, shaking his head angrily as he recalled the delays.

Marcie nodded, remembering in vivid detail the surprisingly frequent times that Ben's small outboard motor had conked out, so they had spent as much time listening to his muttering and tinkering as cruising the lake. If Kirk, a local police officer, hadn't been along to point out his favorite fishing spots and provide stories about growing up in West Windham, the afternoon would have seemed endless instead of just long. Although now that Marcie thought about it, she realized that the motor always seemed to fail right after Kirk had peremptorily ordered Ben to go to a particular spot or had made some derogatory comment about his boating capabilities. She wondered if Ben's mishaps with the boat weren't his passive-aggressive way of getting back at Kirk. Maybe if Kirk hadn't been along, the tour would have gone more smoothly.

The trip had come about when Ben Hanson, the owner of the boat, had sent some photographs and a rather sketchy article to *Roaming New England* describing the Monster of Lake Opal, a strange creature that he claimed inhabited the murky depths of the deep lake. Although most of Ben's photos proved little more than that he needed a better camera, a few were more interesting. If you squinted very hard at them and took an imaginative view, you might possibly see an outline of a long-necked creature that could pass as a cousin of the one in Loch Ness.

In addition to his personal reports, his article, which was only occasionally grammatical, gave an anecdotal history of the monster's sightings based largely on barroom conversations he'd had with long-time residents. It wasn't a very promising beginning, but since the magazine hadn't published any similar stories, Amanda had sent Marcie up to West Windham two days ago to see if there was enough substance in Ben's story to turn it into something usable.

A day of diligent research by Marcie in the local library had established that the legend went back to at least the middle of the nineteenth century. However, sightings had been infrequent in the last fifty years, and the few that had been investigated were dismissed as floating branches or the imaginings of inebriated locals prowling the edge of the lake at twilight. Still, combining her historical research with an abbreviated account of her afternoon spent with Ben on the boat would give Marcie enough material for a short article that would make no claims to have proven much of anything except that New England was filled with quaint folklore.

"Too bad that Ben couldn't have rousted out the monster for us," Marcie said. "In this case a picture is worth a million words."

Kirk frowned. "Good thing he didn't. The old bum would

probably have had a heart attack and the two of us would still be out there trying to fix that piece-of-junk engine."

"Do you think he's ever actually seen the monster like he claims?" Marcie asked. Ben had offered a vivid retelling of an early morning on the lake when the monster had surfaced only an oar's length away. Unfortunately it had been one of the few times Ben was on the lake without his camera.

Kirk snorted. "I think maybe he believes he has, but the guy lives in a world of his own. I wouldn't put much value in anything he says. He's pretty unstable. In my opinion he might even be dangerous."

"Is that why the chief of police suggested that you accompany me?"

When Marcie had checked in at the police station to find out if venturing out on Lake Opal was permitted, Chief Toth had called Kirk in on his day off to go along with her and Ben in the "interest of good community relations," as he put it.

Kirk shrugged his broad shoulders in a way that Marcie found intriguing.

"He hasn't done anything that we can charge him with, but he's definitely off-center. He just showed up about five years ago and got the job as cemetery caretaker because nobody else wanted it. We don't have any information about his past, and he doesn't show up with a criminal record in any of the computer databases I've checked. But all that proves is that so far he's managed to slip through the cracks."

Marcie nodded and put down her menu. She'd decided to go with a salad over the soup, given her sweating problem, and the broiled chicken. Although she'd have preferred the plowman's sixteen-ounce prime rib, that would probably make a bad impression on her date, not to mention his wallet.

"So does Ben really live in the cemetery like he said?" she asked.

"In a small stone house that's been there forever."

"What does he do?" Marcie asked.

"Hard to tell. I guess he's mostly a glorified watchman. He calls himself the grounds supervisor, but the cemetery has a crew that mows the grass and digs the graves. Old Ben just stands around and watches when he isn't off on the lake. He closes the gates of the driveway at sunset and opens them at sunrise. The gates don't keep people out, just cars. So at night he's supposed to make a few rounds through the cemetery to keep trespassers away."

"Do you have many of those?"

"Mostly kids out in the summer looking to scare themselves. Once in a while it gets out of hand with gravestones toppled over, but we don't have as much of that as some of the neighboring towns. Probably because the kids know that crazy Ben is around. Sometimes we've had complaints from parents about Ben threatening the kids, but since the kids are trespassing and Ben has never really attacked anyone, there's nothing much we can do. I figure that it's only a matter of time before he gets in real trouble." Kirk paused for effect. "Plus there are stories . . ."

"What kind of stories?"

Kirk leaned across the table with a mysterious look on his face. Marcie moved closer, as entranced by his wavy brown hair and sparkling white teeth as by what he might have to say.

"Ben has another obsession other than the Monster of Lake Opal."

"What's that?" Marcie asked, unconsciously holding her breath.

"Vampires."

Marcie knew a silly grin had come over her face. That always happened when she heard about something supernatural. A sort of childish excitement resulting from too many horror movies turned her into a gawking adolescent. Since she was close enough to feel Kirk's breath on her cheek, she tried to transform the adolescent grin into something more seductive, but she was afraid that her expression got stuck somewhere around a grimace of pain.

"Are you saying that Ben believes that there are vampires in the cemetery?" she asked.

Kirk sat back and his face became somber. "There're unconfirmed stories, as the chief likes to say."

Marcie thought back to the afternoon spent with the skinny, febrile old man who had cursed his outboard motor as if it were possessed with some kind of malevolent intelligence. There were times when he had seemed pretty normal, if a bit fixated on a questionable legend. And she could tell that he had taken to her. He had made a point of sitting next to her and telling long stories about his times on the lake, even joking with her occasionally to get a laugh. But then there were other times when a funny sensation on the back of her neck caused Marcie to look over and find Ben staring at her in an intense way that she found unnerving.

She reached out and touched Kirk's hand.

"I'm really glad that you were along this afternoon."

"So am I," he replied with a dazzling smile.

"Why don't you tell me some more about what it's like being a police officer in West Windham?"

Now, as Kirk started to speak, Marcie remembered why their conversation on the boat had gone so well. It was because Kirk had done most of the talking.

Chapter Three

Anastasia Narapov, who had introduced herself simply as Mrs. Narapov, looked at the people seated around the table and contorted her face in what seemed to be a valiant effort to smile. She might have been aiming for the benevolent or even maternal. But Amanda thought the resulting spread of the lips fell a bit short of amiable, landing more in the range of the sadly judgmental, as if the woman were girding herself up to do the best she could with a rather motley supply of helpers.

"I hope you are all believers in the next life?" she asked. Her vaguely eastern-European accent made the question sound more like an order.

Martin nodded vigorously, followed by a more timid nod from Bethany, his daughter-in-law, who seemed ready to agree to anything to get the event over with. William frowned, remaining still and silent. Eric Devlin, who had come into the room late as if trying to disassociate himself from the proceedings, seemed not to have heard the question. Amanda smiled politely, indicating that bringing the whole matter up was in slightly poor taste.

"Is it enough that we aren't nonbelievers?" Krow inquired.

Narapov gave a resigned shrug, showing that she was well acquainted with such negativity.

"That's for the spirits to decide," she finally said, giving Martin a disappointed look that told him he had not been careful enough in selecting the evening's participants. "Please hold hands, close your eyes, relax your minds."

Amanda placed her right hand in Krow's. Her left hand had been grasped somewhat tentatively by Eric Devlin, who gave her an apologetic smile. She wasn't certain whether he was apologizing for touching her or for the overall situation. A good-looking man in his late thirties, he had said very little at dinner except when directly addressed by Martin Chastain. She had been rather surprised by this reticence since all the financial advisors Amanda had ever met were excessively gregarious people, overly anxious to sell their services. She wondered if Eric's time was so fully taken up with handling Martin's extensive personal estate that he didn't need to seek more customers.

Never comfortable with closing her eyes in public, Amanda squinted through lowered lashes. Someone turned off the lights, probably Mrs. Ames, so the only light in the room came from a single candle flickering on a sideboard. The table was shrouded in shadows so deep that Amanda could barely make out Bethany's face, even though she was seated directly across from her. As always when ordered to relax, Amanda felt herself grow tense, and Devlin wasn't doing any better if the way his hand was tightly holding hers was any indication. Krow's hand remained relaxed, however, and his breathing had slowed.

They sat like that until Amanda thought she was going to scream from the forced inertia. Then suddenly a low moaning came from Anastasia Narapov's end of the table. Amanda turned her head slightly and peeked, hoping it wouldn't earn her a reprimand. Her pupils had adjusted somewhat to the darkness, and she could see that the medium was gently rocking back and forth in her chair. As she watched, the rocking become increasingly more rapid, although the medium continued to cling to the hands of Martin and William, who sat on either side of her. Just when Amanda thought that the woman's accelerated movements were going to propel her to her feet, she slumped back into the chair, apparently unconscious.

"What do you wish of me?" the woman said a moment later in a voice so deep and masculine that Amanda stared hard, trying to ascertain that her lips were actually moving.

"Is that you, Zaffir?" she asked in her normal tone.

"It is I," the deep voice responded hesitantly as if aroused from sleep. "What do you wish to know?"

"We are trying to contact Larissa Chastain. She will have crossed over six months ago tomorrow."

"You ask much of me. You know how difficult it is to reach those who have only recently arrived."

"I know. But I am asking you to try."

Amanda found herself speculating on why it would be particularly difficult to contact recent arrivals when it must be almost impossible to find any one spirit among all the millions that have crossed over since the beginning. Her mind drifted off into wondering about whether there was a huge heavenly file room or perhaps a super computer of some sort that would allow Zaffir to locate Larissa. She had come to the conclusion that spirits probably would have a form of instant telepathy, when Mrs. Narapov opened her mouth again.

"I am here," a light female voice said.

"Larissa?" Martin asked, with a mixture of joy and worry.

"Don't address the spirit directly," the medium snapped. "She is very fragile, and you could frighten her away."

Amanda could see that everyone's eyes except for Krow's were now open, glancing around, hoping to catch sight of their visitor. But there was nothing to see in the shadowy room.

"Close your eyes and concentrate, or we'll lose her!" Mrs. Narapov demanded. Reluctantly everyone did as ordered, except for Amanda.

"It's me, Martin," Larissa said, apparently willing to skip the intermediary. "Oh, Martin, it's so good to hear your voice again."

"And I yours, my love." He paused for an instant, uncertain what to ask now that the time had come. "Are you happy . . . where you are?"

The medium cleared her throat in a warning fashion.

"Sorry," Martin mumbled.

"Are you happy where you are, my dear?" she repeated.

"Very happy. Everything is peaceful and serene. There is a wonderful sense of love all around me."

Amanda heard a mild snort from the end of the table and wondered if that was William Chastain's comment on such a stereotypical description.

"Ask her . . ." Martin began. "Ask her if she can tell us anything about the person who attacked her."

"She may find that memory very disturbing and leave," Mrs. Narapov warned.

"Please," Martin insisted.

She repeated the question. There was silence for a moment. Then Amanda heard a sound like that of a train whistle coming down the tracks toward her, getting louder and louder. Then it became recognizable as a scream. Amanda opened her eyes fully. The sound escalated until it turned into a shrieking, painful howl. The medium threw her head back, her mouth open wide as if she were baying at the moon. Amanda saw Bethany pull her hands free and clamp them over her ears. Devlin's hand clenched hard on hers, and Amanda was sure she was clinging to his as well. Krow's hand remained firm but didn't tighten. She glanced sideways at him for reassurance, but he continued to face straight ahead with his eyes closed, waiting patiently for what came next.

Finally the shrieking stopped, leaving the room intensely quiet. After a long pause, Martin opened his mouth to speak, but the medium held up her hand for silence.

"If Larissa hasn't left, she will speak again in her own time."

Everyone around the table seemed to be holding their breath, dreading a repetition of the tormented sound.

"I cannot speak directly of the one who tore me from your world," Larissa said in a voice that sounded weak and very far away. "The wound is still too fresh."

"She's fading," Mrs. Narapov warned. "New spirits can't stay in this world very long."

"Ask her if she can at least give us a clue as to who the

murderer is?" Martin asked, the urgency obvious in his voice.

The medium repeated the question. Everyone now stared into the darkness, waiting for a reply.

"Ask her again," Martin demanded as the silence lengthened.

"Look inside my coffin," Larissa suddenly answered, her voice so loud and angry that she could have been sitting at the table with them. "You will discover the identity of the guilty one if you look inside my coffin."

With a dramatic sigh, Mrs. Narapov slumped back into the chair and went limp.

"Are you all right?" Martin asked a moment later, reaching over to pat her shoulder.

The woman's lids flickered, then opened. She straightened up in the chair. "The séance for tonight is over," she announced in a remarkably firm voice.

As the lights came back on, Amanda realized that somewhere along the way she had released her grip on Eric Devlin's hand. He was sitting there blinking and looking slightly dazed, as was everyone else except for Mrs. Narapov and Krow, who turned to Amanda and smiled.

"I promised you a good show, didn't I?" he said, leaning close to her and whispering softly.

"Are they always this way?" Amanda asked weakly, still feeling a bit off balance.

"No, this one was really something special."

"You mean because of the scream."

Krow shook his head. "No, that's pretty typical. All these old-fashioned mediums have an amazing command of their voices."

"So what was so special?"

He turned to look directly at her, and Amanda noted that he did seem genuinely puzzled, not an expression that she could remember ever having seen on his face before.

He lowered his voice so that the others couldn't hear. "What surprised me is that Larissa gave us such specific instructions. Usually the spirits are frustratingly vague in the way they express themselves. A skeptic would say that it's the medium's way of not being proven wrong. If the message is open to a variety of interpretations, it can never be conclusively disproven. But saying that we would find a clue in the coffin is pretty specific."

"Of course, we still don't know what to look for in the coffin," Amanda pointed out.

"And we may never find out unless Martin tries to have it opened."

Martin's suddenly raised voice silenced all the others in the room. Amanda turned and saw that he was standing toe to toe with his son, his face was red and his body almost shaking with agitation.

"Do you think I care what people will think?"

"I'm just saying that this will get around. If people hear that you're going to séances and then opening Larissa's coffin, it could hurt the company."

"*My* company, I remind you, William," Martin said, his tone getting louder. "And it will remain mine as long as I am alive. And if you think that I have any intention of not doing everything I can to see that Larissa's murderer is brought to justice, then you are sadly mistaken."

William turned on his heel and left the room. After glancing around nervously as if uncertain whether to be rude,

Bethany finally gave an embarrassed smile then turned and hurried after him.

"The first thing tomorrow I'll call my lawyer to find out what I have to do to have Larissa's coffin opened," Martin said to Mrs. Narapov, who nodded casually, as if opening coffins was a common occurrence.

Krow leaned close to Amanda's ear. "Well, I guess we may find out what's in that coffin after all," he whispered.

Chapter Four

"**I** don't want to go in there, Jared. Besides, I have to be home by ten because I've got *her* with me," said Tami, giving her twelve-year-old sister, Karen, a disgusted look.

Karen stuck her tongue out at her older sister. She knew it was too dark for Tami to see, but it made her feel better anyway. Even though Tami was five years older, Karen knew that she was the smarter. Karen put up with the constant bullying and sarcastic remarks from her older sister because she was convinced that in ten years' time Tami would be living in near poverty with five kids and a husband like Jared, who, in Karen's opinion, was a borderline mental defective. By then Karen was confident that she would have a degree from an excellent college and be well on her way to starting a successful career somewhere more interesting than West Windham.

"C'mon," Jared said, reaching out and grabbing Tami's

arm. "If we cut through the cemetery, we'll come out near your house. You'll make it home faster that way."

"I don't want to go in there," the girl said, pulling away.

"Why? Are you afraid of the dead?" Jared gave a poor imitation of a spooky laugh.

Tami cringed. "You're not funny. What about that guy who hangs out in there?"

"Old Ben? He's harmless." Jared stuck his chest out. "All I'd have to do is go boo and he'd scurry off like a frightened rabbit."

"You always want to have things your own way," Tami said, bringing up one of her frequent complaints.

By the glow of the streetlight Karen could see that an expression of sulky stubbornness had settled on her sister's face. She knew this would soon lead to a lengthy and embarrassing conversation as Jared tried to put her back in a good mood and Tami demanded more proof that he really cared about her. All this was more than Karen felt she could bear, especially on a chilly March night.

"We could walk through the cemetery in the time it's taking us to decide," Karen said, easily slipping between the iron railings next to the gatepost and going into the cemetery. She set off at a brisk pace along the path that the cars used.

"Karen, where are you going?" Tami called out in distress.

Karen ignored her and kept walking.

"Hey, slow down!" Jared shouted as he slid through the fence as well. When he reached Karen's side, he began to walk along next to her.

"It's dark in here," he said.

Karen said nothing, thinking that was too obvious to deserve a comment.

He fumbled in his pocket and took out a small flashlight.

"I always carry this with me," he said proudly, as if that entitled him to an award.

Tami quickly made her way through the fence and ran to catch up with them. She grabbed Karen by the arm. "What are you doing, you idiot!"

"I'm trying to get home by ten, so *you* won't get in trouble," Karen said calmly. "Now do you want to stand here talking about it and get grounded, or do we get a move on?"

Tami paused and glanced around at the dark silhouettes of the headstones that surrounded them like a silent army. Jared swung the narrow beam of his flashlight in a wide circle.

"See, no ghosts or vampires," he announced with a grin. "At least not right here."

"Jerk," Tami muttered. "Okay, let's go. But no slowing down. I want to get out of here fast."

With Jared leading, they made their way over a small hill. The lights from the street didn't reach that far, and soon they were completely dependent on the small flashlight. The intermittent traffic noise also disappeared, leaving only Tami's short, jagged breaths to break the silence, as even Jared seemed to have run out of comments.

"What's that over there?" Jared stopped so quickly that both Karen and Tami ran into his back.

"What? Where?" Tami asked, nervously swiveling to look around her.

Jared pointed into the darkness with his flashlight. "Don't you see a light over there?"

Karen stared in the direction of the flashlight beam. Past several rows of stones, she could just make out a faint rectangular glow that seemed to be coming from a doorway of some kind. She blinked twice to make sure it wasn't an optical illusion, but it didn't disappear.

"Let's check it out," Jared said, diving off the road.

"Are you crazy?" Tami whispered loudly. "I'm staying right here."

"Afraid of ghosts?" Jared taunted.

"Who knows what's over there? It could be some psycho just waiting to kill people."

"Suit yourself. But I've got the flashlight." He left the path and headed in the direction of the light.

"I think we're safer with Jared and the flashlight than stumbling along by ourselves," Karen said to her sister, following him off the road.

"Wait for me!" Tami called out a second later, rushing to catch up with her.

When they were about twenty feet away from the light, Jared stopped to study the situation. The glow was definitely coming from inside a small stone building.

"What do they call a place like that?"

"A mausoleum," Karen said. "It's a place where they keep bodies."

"I thought they buried them in the ground?"

"Some families sort of store them in one of those buildings."

"Guess they don't rot as fast that way."

"I don't know. Maybe it just seems nicer to have them above ground if you want to visit," Karen suggested.

"In the middle of the night?" Jared asked.

Karen paused and decided that Jared wasn't quite as stupid as she had thought.

"I doubt it."

"Maybe it's a graverobber," Tami whispered. "I've heard that there are people who steal bodies."

Jared softly cleared his throat. "Well, I guess I'll have to check it out."

"Why?" Karen asked. "We could call the police. I've got my cell phone."

"They aren't going to believe a bunch of kids," Jared replied. "And if someone is in there, he'll probably be long gone by the time the police show up. We have to check it out now."

Deciding that he was just showing off to impress her sister, Karen kept quiet.

"Don't be stupid," Tami said hoarsely. "You don't know what could be in there."

"Whatever it is, I'll bet it's no ghost." Jared tried to laugh at his own joke, but it came out more as a high-pitched giggle.

As though annoyed with his voice for betraying him, he immediately turned away from the girls and headed toward the open mausoleum door.

"Idiot!" Tami hissed at his back.

"You're just making it worse," Karen said.

"Am not," she responded but sounded doubtful.

"Let's follow him a little way," Karen suggested after they'd watched Jared slowly make his way closer to the building.

"Why?" Tami asked. "Just because he doesn't care about

what happens to himself doesn't mean that we have to be stupid."

"He might need our help," Karen said, realizing for the first time that along with stupidity, cowardice was another of her older sister's failings.

"He's on his own. I'm staying right here," Tami said. But when Karen walked toward the mausoleum, she tagged along, apparently more afraid of being left alone than of what they might find.

As Karen got closer, she could see that only one side of the double doors of the mausoleum was open. The light shining inside was faint, as if it were coming from a large flashlight rather than from a kerosene lantern like the ones her family took on camping trips.

Jared paused for a moment, as if screwing up his courage. He glanced back at her. She waved to offer him support, then wondered if he could even see her standing in the darkness. He plunged through the doorway. It took a moment for Karen to realize that the light that had been on inside the building had suddenly gone out, so there was only the flicker of Jared's small flashlight.

"I think someone's in there."

"Oh, God," Tami said. "Let's get out of here."

Not even bothering to reply, Karen began cautiously walking forward until she was about six feet from the open door. She stood there for several moments trying to decide whether to follow Jared inside. Just as she was about to take a step forward, the beam of his flashlight began coming toward her and a figure appeared in the doorway.

"Is that you, Jared?" Karen asked, needing all of her willpower not to run.

"Yeah," he said weakly.

Recognizing his voice, she breathed a sigh of relief. Then the flashlight in his right hand seemed to jump around until it finally pointed up at his face. His left hand was behind his head as if he was trying to remember something. When he brought his hand down, he focused the light on it as if he had never seen it before. Karen saw that his hand was dark.

"What's that?" she asked.

Instead of answering, Jared fell forward, reaching out to grab her shoulder for support. His fingers only brushed her arm, but even that was enough to almost push her over. For a moment she wasn't really aware of anything, then she heard Tami screaming right behind her. Fortunately, the screaming grew faint as Tami began to run back in the direction of the road.

Karen picked up the flashlight from where it had rolled and focused the beam of light on the back of Jared's head. His hair was already thickly matted with blood. She heard a noise near the building, and brought the beam of light up just in time to see a dark figure dart off among the headstones. Then Karen took out her cell phone and, pleased to see that her hand hardly shook at all, she dialed 911.

Chapter Five

M arcie was already sitting in the restaurant at the West Windham Inn, tucking into a short stack of blueberry pancakes when Amanda came down the next morning. Before she'd started working with Amanda six months before, Marcie would have gone with the full order of five pancakes plus sausage. But working with someone as slim and stylish as Amanda was forcing her to think more about her appearance. Not that Amanda would ever have directly said anything, but the force of example was enough. Marcie had also found that since she had been working for *Roaming New England,* her desire to eat between meals had declined dramatically. She figured that being happy with her life had a lot to do with it.

She and Amanda had connected only briefly at the inn late yesterday before they went off to their respective dinner engagements, so Marcie was looking forward to having a chance to tell Amanda about her experiences hunting for the Monster of Lake Opal. Not to mention her date with Kirk. When Amanda came into the dining room, Marcie gave her a welcoming wave to catch her attention.

"Good morning," Amanda mumbled as she approached the table.

"Good morning," Marcie replied in an intentionally soft voice. She knew that Amanda never really woke up until after her first cup of coffee, and nothing disturbed her more than being greeted with the exuberance of someone who had already been out for an invigorating morning run.

The waitress came over, poured coffee in Amanda's cup, and took her order of a soft-boiled egg and dry rye toast. After Amanda swallowed a long gulp of coffee, she gave a tentative smile as if checking to see whether her face might shatter, and then began to gingerly rub her forehead. Marcie commented that she seemed even a bit slower off the mark than usual.

"After the séance Nick insisted that we stop downstairs in the bar and talk over what happened. I only had one white wine, but when I got to bed, I had trouble sleeping. I don't know whether it was the wine or the séance."

Marcie knew that Amanda's father had been an alcoholic, so she was always careful to limit her drinking and suspicious of its effects.

"I hope Nick didn't try driving back to Portland after drinking a lot," Marcie said. "The roads out here are pretty dark at night."

"He only had two drinks, and he got a room at the inn."

"Oh, he did, did he," Marcie said in a fluttery voice, twisting her face into a ridiculously lecherous grin. "If only I'd known."

"Spare me the theatrics," Amanda said with a faint smile. "I'm in no mood to emote."

"The coffee will help," Marcie assured her. "Anyhow, you're the one Nick is interested in, not me."

Amanda sipped her coffee and said nothing about Nick, which was what Marcie expected. Amanda was six years older and more experienced, and she didn't like to reveal much about her personal life. So Marcie had been surprised two weeks ago when Amanda had confided to her that Jeff, her boyfriend of the last six months, was moving to Washington and wanted her to go with him. When Marcie had asked whether she was planning to go along, Amanda had shrugged. However, the casualness had seemed forced, at odds with the concerned expression on her face. Marcie was still on tenterhooks about whether her boss and closest friend in the area would soon to be leaving, but she was afraid to press the matter.

"How did the séance go?" she asked.

Amanda gave her a summary of the evening.

Marcie's eyes grew wide. "Wow! I wish I'd been there."

Amanda smiled. Even after nine months on the job Marcie still got excited at the prospect of experiencing something paranormal. Not that any of the stories they'd investigated so far had resulted in hard evidence supporting the existence of the supernatural. However, Amanda had to admit that Marcie's almost childlike enthusiasm was what made the "Weird Happenings" column work as well as it did. Her energy and willingness to believe was easily transmitted to the public in her writing.

Amanda knew that was one of the major differences between them. Although not quite as skeptical as Nick, she was just as happy to find a natural explanation for the apparently extraordinary, while Marcie longed for some kind of unexplained experience to sweep her away. Marcie's constant quest to find the mystery around the next corner gave the column a vibrancy that attracted readers.

"It wasn't *that* exciting," Amanda said, although she knew that it actually had been at the time.

"A ghost appeared."

"A ghost didn't *appear,*" Amanda corrected her patiently. "Mrs. Narapov simply modulated her voice to sound like Larissa Chastain."

"Did her husband believe it sounded like her?"

Amanda nodded. "That's what he thought, anyway. But as Nick pointed out to me in the bar last night, people believe what they want to believe and hear what they want to hear. Larissa might have honked like a goose in real life, but her husband would swear that the sweet, faint sounds of last night were exact replicas."

"But still," Marcie insisted with a trace of stubbornness, "the ghost did answer his question."

"I suppose."

Amanda sipped more coffee as her order arrived, then slowly began to chew on a piece of toast. Marcie virtually inhaled her food, while Amanda made it into a meditation practice. So when they ate together, Marcie was always done with her usually sizeable meal well before Amanda had put more than the tiniest dent in her morsel.

"But it wasn't a very direct answer, when you think about it," Amanda pointed out, picking up the conversational thread again. "I mean, if you'd been murdered and came back to chat with people, wouldn't the first thing you said be something clear like 'Jim did it. Book him'?"

Marcie grinned. "Yeah, I guess I would. But maybe there are rules for ghosts like there are for doctors. They can't tell you things directly but have to give you a lot of mumbo jumbo."

Amanda and Marcie sat eating in silence for a few more minutes. Marcie was soon finished and sat sipping her third cup of coffee.

"How did your date with Kirk go?" Amanda asked as she started on her second cup.

"Pretty well," Marcie said, trying to keep the excitement out of her voice. "It took us a little while to break the old conversational ice. He's not the world's biggest talker, but once we got on the subject of Ben Hanson and the monster things picked up."

"The Monster of Lake Opal doesn't exactly sound like romantic dinner conversation."

Marcie gave her a lopsided grin. "It was the one thing we had in common after all, and you have to start somewhere. By the way, it turns out that Ben isn't just known around here for his stories about the monster. He's also got quite a reputation as a believer in vampires."

Amanda crooked a critical eyebrow as Marcie went on to explain about Ben's cemetery wanderings. When Marcie was done, Amanda carefully replaced her cup in its saucer and tapped a polished fingernail on the tabletop.

"I realize that you've already put a lot of time into this Lake Opal story, but maybe we should drop the whole idea," Amanda said. "To me this is starting to sound like the ravings of a guy who's seriously delusional. If we publish this, it will just encourage every lunatic in New England to polish up their hallucinations and pop them in the mail to us."

"There have been other sightings than Ben's," Marcie pointed out.

"But nothing significant in the last fifty years, that's what you said yesterday, right?"

"True."

"I suppose we could run it as a folklore piece. We could credit Ben as a source, but not mention his supposed sightings at all."

"But somehow that doesn't seem right either," Marcie objected. "Ben is the one who contacted us. It really is his story."

Amanda gave her friend a shrewd look. "You sort of like this old guy, don't you?"

Marcie nodded. "He was nice to me. He treated me like his granddaughter. I guess I also feel a little sorry for him."

"Well, if you've got enough material for a column, we'll talk about it back at the office. We can run it by Greg," she said, referring to Greg Sheffield, the managing editor.

"We're going back today?"

"We really should. I have a few things to finish on the June issue before it goes to press."

Marcie nodded. It had been a bit disconcerting when she had started working on a monthly magazine to discover that you were always planning at least four months in advance. Here it was the middle of March and they were almost finished with June.

"I'm sorry you won't have more time to get to know Kirk. What's his last name?"

"Ames."

Amanda paused. "I met a Mrs. Ames last night at the Chastain house."

"That's his mother. She's worked as the housekeeper there for years."

"Anyway, what I wanted to say is that it's only about an hour and a half at the most from Wells to here. That wouldn't make a relationship impossible. Making him travel might even be a way of testing his level of commitment," Amanda said with a small smile.

The offices of *Roaming New England* occupied an old house in Wells, Maine, right along Route 1. It wasn't lavish quarters, but the view of the ocean from her desk was one that Amanda found herself missing whenever she was away for very long. There was something reassuring about the openness of the water, especially in contrast to the closed, forest-filled darkness of the interior of upper New England.

"I don't think we're quite at the commitment-for-life stage yet," Marcie said. "We're more at the getting-to-know-you stage."

She tried to make her voice sound light, but when Kirk had driven her back to the inn at around nine, their conversation in the car had somehow moved on to a series of ardent kisses. And the disappointed expression on Kirk's face when she firmly wished him goodnight had indicated that he didn't want the evening to end so early. Reliving everything in her mind had kept her from getting to sleep until after midnight.

"Another advantage to being at a distance is that if it doesn't work out, you won't keep running into each other at the supermarket every week," Amanda said.

"Has that ever happened to you?" Marcie asked, prying in spite of herself into Amanda's personal history.

Instead of answering, Amanda's gaze traveled across the room to the entrance to the restaurant.

"Does your friend Kirk have short brown hair, a granite chin, and a muscular body?"

"Yes."

"Does he look good in a police uniform?"

"He was off-duty yesterday at the lake. I've never seen him in uniform."

"Turn around and I think you will."

Marcie turned and saw Kirk standing at the lobby entrance to the restaurant. He was saying something to the hostess and pointing in the direction of Marcie and Amanda. Next to him was a rounder, older man whom Marcie recognized as Roger Toth, the chief of police. Nodding in a friendly way to the hostess, the chief navigated across the restaurant to their table with a rolling, almost nautical gait that somehow managed to just keep him from bumping into the closely placed tables.

"Would you ladies allow us to join you?" he asked, stopping by their table and surveying the room with a quick glance to make sure that no one was within easy eavesdropping distance.

Amanda nodded her agreement, and Marcie quickly performed the introductions while the two men drew over chairs from a nearby table and sat down. Marcie gave Kirk a friendly nod. The one he gave in return was rather stiff, telling her this was a business visit and not a getting-to-know-you-better call. This was reinforced when he took out a spiral notebook and a pen, obviously preparing to take notes.

The chief sat down in the chair with a sigh and put his hat in his lap, staring down at it for a moment as if its familiarity would help him focus.

"We had an incident last night in the West Windham cemetery," he began. "A teenage boy was attacked around nine-thirty when he apparently surprised a vandal in one of the mausoleums. It was the mausoleum of the Chastain family."

"Was the boy seriously injured?" Amanda asked, her training as a newspaper reporter taking over.

"He has a concussion. They're keeping him in the hospital for observation."

"Was he able to identify his attacker?"

The chief shook his head sadly. "He mumbled something to the EMTs about going into the mausoleum and someone in the shadows hitting him on the back of the head. I'll talk to him more later on today, but I don't hold out much hope that he saw anything useful. There were two girls with him. One was in hysterics and couldn't tell us much of anything. The younger one said she saw someone come out of the mausoleum and run off, but she didn't get a good enough look to describe him. The attacker also must have taken away the weapon that was used. At least we didn't find it."

"What was he doing in the mausoleum?" Amanda asked.

"Well, the intruder had taken the lid off the crypt so he could get at the coffin, but the coffin was still closed. Probably the boy disturbed him before he could pry it open."

"How did he get into the mausoleum in the first place?" Amanda asked.

"We think the lock on the doors must have been broken at some time in the past, because they were padlocked together with a chain. We found a cut chain lying on the ground."

Amanda nodded. "Have you talked to Martin Chastain about what happened?"

"We called the family the first thing this morning to tell them, but Mr. Chastain had already left for work. Apparently he had an early morning meeting. We spoke to Mrs. Ames."

"The housekeeper," Amanda said, suppressing a smile at the thought that the woman had probably introduced herself that way.

"And Kirk here's mother," he said, quickly holding up his hand to silence Amanda as she opened her mouth to ask yet another question. He took a deep breath. "It's what she told us that gave me the idea of seeing you. She seemed to think that the vandalism at the mausoleum might be related to what happened at the séance. Something about a clue being in the coffin. But Mrs. Ames hadn't actually been in the room at the time. When I mentioned it to my deputy here, he told me Ms. Ducasse had told him that you were going to be attending the séance. So I figured that maybe you could supply me with the details."

The chief folded his hands across his wide stomach and gave her a patient smile that said he was glad to have finally gotten in a question and was willing to wait to hear her answer.

"I can tell you everything I know with the help of that man," Amanda said, pointing at Nick Krow, who had just entered the dining room and was approaching their table.

"Good morning," Nick said, keeping his eyes on Amanda for some hint of what was going on. "Am I interrupting official business?"

"Why don't you join us, Professor Krow?" the chief said after Amanda had performed the introductions. "I gather from Mrs. Ames that you were at last night's séance as well."

Krow pulled up a chair and sat next to Amanda. The chief

explained again his need for information, and between the two of them, Amanda and Nick gave him a summary of what had occurred the evening before.

"So the . . . ah . . . ghost told Chastain to look in his wife's coffin to find out who had murdered her?" the chief asked when they were through.

"Right," Krow said, grinning slightly at the chief's discomfort with having to quote a ghost's testimony.

"But there were no specifics as to what to look for?"

"No." Nick's eyes widened slightly. "Are you thinking that someone decided to check out the coffin for the clue before Martin had it opened?"

"What time did the séance end?"

"Around eight-fifteen," Nick said, glancing at Amanda who nodded agreement.

"It does seem to be a bit of a coincidence that the two events occurred so close together," the chief replied dryly.

"That means you think the person who attacked the boy was someone who had been at the séance?" Krow asked.

"Or someone who was told about what went on there."

"And that someone would be the murderer of Larissa Chastain?"

"Could be, if you believe a ghost," the chief said with a smile. "But I've learned not to travel too far without some real evidence to help me along."

"Chief, were you involved in the investigation of Larissa Chastain's death?" Amanda asked.

"Nope. The Portland police ran that investigation, but they sent me a copy of their preliminary report because the victim lived in town."

"Did they have any suspects?"

He shook his head. "The case is still open, but they pretty much concluded that it was a mugging gone wrong. Mrs. Chastain must have struggled when someone tried to take her purse and got hit on the head for her troubles."

"I'm sure they must have checked on the husband's whereabouts at the time," said Nick. "Isn't the husband always the prime suspect when his wife is murdered?"

"Martin Chastain was at work at the time, although they couldn't find anyone who could actually say with certainty that they had seen him there around the time of the murder. I gather he worked alone in his private office, which has its own entrance."

"Did he have a motive?" Amanda asked.

"By all accounts Martin adored his wife," the chief replied. "At least the Portland police couldn't find anyone who thought differently. On the other hand, William Chastain, the son, is another matter. He also lacked an alibi for the exact time of death and did have a motive."

"He didn't like his stepmother?" asked Marcie.

"Hard to tell if it was personal or more financial," the chief answered. "William seems to have felt that Larissa married his father for his money."

"I'd have thought that a rich man like Martin would have had a prenuptial agreement," said Amanda.

The chief cleared his throat slowly, as if uncertain how much more he wanted to tell them about the investigation.

"None of this is for publication, chief," Amanda assured him. "And since we know the people involved, it's possible that we could be of some assistance."

"Actually I *was* going to ask you for a bit of help," the

chief paused, then seemed to make the decision to take them into his confidence. "Look, keep it to yourselves, but Larissa would have gotten a flat payment of one hundred thousand dollars if she and Martin divorced unless she had been unfaithful. Under those circumstances she would have gotten nothing. The more important matter, however, is that according to the housekeeper Martin wanted to have another child. And if that had happened, then William's inheritance would most likely have been cut in half."

"So William had the best motive and no alibi," Amanda said.

"But there was also no evidence to indicate that he committed the crime," the chief added.

"I've known Will for a long time," Krow said. "I'd find it hard to believe that he's a murderer."

"It's always hard to imagine that of anyone you know personally," the chief pointed out.

"How would you like us to help you?" Amanda asked turning to the chief, who, clearly uncomfortable, looked down and studied his hat some more.

"According to what Ms. Ducasse told my officer yesterday, you aren't friends with Martin Chastain. Is that true?"

"I'd never met him before yesterday," Amanda affirmed.

"What about you, Professor Krow?" the chief said, giving the man a sharp look.

"I'd never met him before either, but I've known Will since we were in college together."

"Would that keep you from helping me?"

Nick considered the question for a moment, then shook his head. "If it does become a problem, I'll let you know."

The chief cleared his throat slowly in preparation. "Well, you see, the thing is this: I don't really know Martin Chastain either. Oh, I know him by sight. After all he's lived here in town a dog's age, but I wouldn't say that I really know him. I've met William a couple of times at public events. He seems like a regular guy, but I can't say much more than that. And the big thing is I wasn't there last night at the séance." The chief paused and tapped his hat lightly on his knee. "I'm also no expert on this supernatural stuff. So I thought that since you aren't particularly close to him and know more about this kind of thing than I do, it might be helpful if one or both of you came along as sort of informal consultants when I talk to Mr. Chastain. He's an important man around here, even if he does pretty much keep to himself."

"Isn't it a little unusual to have civilians involved in a criminal case?" asked Amanda.

"Sure is, and I'm not real happy about it," the chief said. "But you have to admit that this is a pretty unusual case, what with the ghosts and all. Plus when I called the Portland police to tell them about all this, I mentioned your names, and it seems the chief of detectives there is willing to vouch for Professor Krow."

Amanda gave Nick a quizzical look, but he didn't meet her eye.

"I was planning to go back to Wells this morning," Amanda said. Nick turned toward her, and she could see that he was about to launch into an argument to convince her to stay, so she hurried on. "But I guess that I can spare one more day if it will help solve a crime."

"I'm in," Nick added.

"Good, good," the chief said, bobbing his head up and

down with satisfaction. "And maybe Ms. Ducasse would be willing to spend some more time with my Officer Ames here while he visits Ben Hanson to find out where he was last night. He never put in an appearance at the cemetery, even after all the commotion started. According to Kirk, Ben liked you. He can be a prickly guy at times, and having you there might make a visit from the police go down a little better."

"How is Hanson involved in all this? I thought he spent his time cruising around Lake Opal looking for the monster," Krow said.

"Ben lives in the cemetery," Marcie explained. "He's sort of a guard and groundskeeper."

"Does he see monsters in the cemetery too?" Nick asked half-facetiously.

Marcie caught Kirk's eye.

"Actually he sees vampires," Kirk said closing his notebook and speaking for the first time.

"Hmm, who would have thought there was so much paranormal activity in one small town," Nick said, giving Amanda a sidelong smile.

"Who indeed," she replied.

"Well, I'm hoping that there isn't any," the chief said, climbing to his feet with a sigh. "I'm hoping we find that all this is nothing more than normal, wholesome criminal activity."

Chapter Six

"What do you want?" Ben Hanson said, blocking the doorway. He stared at Kirk with a hostile expression, as if he hardly recognized him as the same young man who had been on his boat yesterday.

"I wanted to come by to thank you for all the help you gave me," Marcie said, stepping in front of the officer. "I've got enough to write up the story, and I'll be sending you a copy in a couple of weeks."

Ben's eyes focused on her and his face softened into a smile. "That's nice of you. I'll look forward to reading it."

"Do you mind if we come in a minute?" she asked.

"The place is a mess, but if you want to all right," Ben said, stepping back into the building.

The outside of the house reminded Marcie of something out of the Middle Ages, with its thick, rough-hewn stone exterior, casement windows, and green tile roof. The front room, however, had a more finished look with white plaster walls and gleaming hardwood floors. Hardly a mess by any normal definition, it looked clean but austere, with a small sofa and several institutional-looking chairs grouped around the large stone fireplace that filled one wall of the room. A couple of pine tables stood along the other walls. It took a moment for Marcie to realize that what struck her as strange about the room was its anonymity. She attributed this to the lack of any pictures on the walls or photos on the tables. The splayed-open magazines and piled-up newspapers that seemed to sprout up automatically in every place that Marcie had ever lived were also completely absent.

Ben took one of the chairs and motioned them toward the sofa. The sofa was really little more than a love seat, and as she sat down, Marcie was suddenly very aware that her hips were touching Kirk's. Deciding that this wasn't the time for quite so much intimacy, she scooted as far away as possible and managed to open up a small space between them.

"You're probably aware of the incident that took place here last night," Kirk said and paused, waiting for Ben to nod. All he got was a blank expression, so he went on, "A boy was attacked."

"Whereabouts?" Ben asked, sliding forward to perch on the edge of his chair, as if expecting to have to run off at any moment.

"Inside the Chastain mausoleum."

"How'd he get in? The doors are all chained up."

"The chain was cut."

Ben pressed down hard on the wooden arms of his chair. Marcie noticed how the ropelike muscles of his slender arms tensed and realized he was probably a lot stronger than he looked. He was thin to the point of emaciation, and Marcie wondered if he had enough to eat or if he spent his probably small salary on alcohol or drugs.

"How come you weren't out doing your rounds last night?" Kirk asked sharply.

Ben gave them a slack-jawed grin. It was such a sudden change of expression that it almost seemed like he was trying to convince them that he was dim-witted.

"I was so tired last night when I got back from our jaunt around the lake that I turned in early. I guess I didn't hear a thing."

"Did you turn in after spending some time with the bottle?" Kirk asked.

Ben gave another loose grin.

"Maybe. There's no law against drinking a little too much in your own home, is there?"

"The boy's got a concussion, but it looks like he'll make it," Marcie said, deciding that it was a good time to intervene to prevent an argument.

Ben nodded, then gazed off into the distance, clearly thinking about something else.

"Do you have any idea why anyone would break into the Chastain mausoleum?" asked Marcie.

Ben licked his lips as if about to speak, then shook his head.

"It couldn't have been you out there last night, could it?" Kirk asked.

"Not me. I was asleep like I told you. But if I did want to get into that mausoleum, it would be easy. I have a key to the padlock. Only Mr. Chastain and I have keys. So I wouldn't have the need to cut any chain."

"Have you seen anyone wandering around the cemetery recently?" asked Marcie, still sensing that Ben was holding something back.

"Not recently."

Marcie smiled to try to reassure him. "No, but on some other night—maybe you saw something on a night when you did make your rounds."

His eyes slid away from hers, and he shook his head.

"Not even a vampire," Kirk said.

"You wouldn't make fun like that if you'd seen some of the things I have."

Kirk got up and walked across to Ben. He stood right in front of him, staring down at the seated man. "Anything spooky you've seen was in the bottom of a bottle."

Ben opened his mouth then paused. "I've seen lots of things," he finally said, staring at the floor.

"When did you last walk past the mausoleum in the day time?" Marcie asked as Kirk stalked over to the fireplace, dramatically shaking his head in disgust.

Ben frowned. "Guess I've been by within the last few days. Since all the snow melted anyway, that would be about a week ago."

"Was the mausoleum chained shut?"

"Sure."

"Would you have noticed?" Kirk asked from the far side of the room.

"I'm sure I would have noticed if it wasn't."

"We're done here," Kirk said abruptly, walking quickly back across the room and positioning himself again in front of the older man who shrank back into the chair. "I hope you've been telling us the truth. Your job could be on the line here. And if you lost your job, then you'd lose all this." He gestured to indicate the house.

"I'm telling the truth," Ben said sullenly.

"Thank you for your help," Marcie said.

Ben nodded briefly, but his eyes were dull. He didn't stand up when they left the room.

"You were kind of hard on him, weren't you?" Marcie said to Kirk as they walked back to the patrol car.

Kirk took off his hat and ran a hand gingerly over his short, spiky hair as if the points hurt.

"I'm sorry if I upset you, Marcie. But it's the only way to be with guys like that. They never tell you the truth unless you scare it out of them. You've got to show them who's boss before you can get anywhere."

Marcie had heard *that* phrase plenty of times before. Her father, who was borderline abusive, never seemed to tire of telling her how you had to intimidate people to get them to do what they were supposed to do. Career military, he had been passed over for promotion repeatedly because his superiors thought he didn't know how to get the best out of his men by means of positive motivation. Her father never accepted their criticism and constantly complained about how soft the Army had become. "I'd rather be feared than loved," he'd repeat like a mantra, to ward off his feelings of failure.

"I have some paperwork to do back at the office," Kirk said as he was driving Marcie back to the inn. "But how about we get together around one o'clock for some lunch?"

"Sorry, I can't make it. I have some work to do on the magazine."

"Maybe tonight for dinner?"

"I think Amanda will probably want to meet with me, so I'd better not make any commitment."

Kirk gave a shrug that seemed casual, but a look of irritation mixed with disappointment flashed across his face.

"Okay, whatever," he said.

He probably doesn't get turned down very often, Marcie thought, completely amazed that she was the one doing it.

Chapter Seven

Mrs. Ames opened the door and stared at them, as if wondering why they were cluttering up her front step in the middle of a busy morning.

"We're here to see Martin Chastain," the chief said. "We called him at work and arranged to meet him here."

Without saying a word, she stepped back out of the doorway, apparently her economical way of telling them to enter.

"Wait in there. I'll get Mr. Chastain," she said, pointing toward the open door to the living room where the séance had been held the night before.

The chief led the way and walked into the room. He went directly over to the round table.

"So this is where you all sat last night?" he asked.

"That's right," Krow replied.

"Doesn't look very spooky," the chief said, surveying the room.

Amanda had to agree. Even though the dark wood and heavy drapes still gave the place a subdued look, the light pouring in through the space between the drapes brightened the room and made the events of last night seem distant and ephemeral. She could see why mediums preferred to work evenings. A shadowy atmosphere made voices from the next world more convincing. *A medium would probably say that darkness was more conducive to contacting the spirit world, but perhaps,* Amanda thought, *it simply made the participants more susceptible to deception.*

"Most so-called paranormal events are a matter of atmospherics," Nick said, reading her mind. "They don't work well under the glow of florescent lights."

"There was still the message," the chief objected. "That was clear enough in any light."

"And maybe frightening enough to motivate someone to try to break into Larissa's coffin, especially if that someone had murdered Larissa Chastain," Krow agreed.

Amanda turned from where she was studying one of the landscape paintings on the wall.

"But you're assuming that the killer would believe the message. I'm no expert in crime, but I would guess that most murderers are pretty cool customers. Would a message from the great beyond instantly get him running around the cemetery at night?"

The chief frowned. "I suppose it all depends. I've known my share of criminals. Some of them are surprisingly superstitious. There was one thief who always carried the rabbit's foot his father had given him whenever he went out to commit a burglary. He lost it in a bar one night and during his next job we caught him. He swore that we'd never have gotten him if he hadn't lost his good luck charm."

"Even if Larissa's killer wasn't superstitious, he might have just been playing it safe," Nick said. "Checking to see if there was a clue of some kind."

Amanda nodded, still doubtful as Martin Chastain walked into the room.

"Was my wife's coffin opened?" he asked immediately.

The chief paused for a minute, somewhat taken aback by the question.

"Well, the lid of the container that held the casket had been lifted off, but as far as we can tell, the casket was unopened, and there were no signs of pry marks on the wood."

"That doesn't mean anything. The casket wasn't sealed. My wife had a fear of being buried alive."

"But wasn't she embalmed?" Krow asked.

"Of course. Her fear was irrational, but I abided by her wishes nonetheless."

"Wouldn't putting her coffin in a stone container go against her wishes as well?" Krow asked.

"The container is constructed of a heavy plastic that's made to look like stone and relatively easy to lift off." Chastain paused and smiled weakly. "I know this sounds like an odd coincidence, but Larissa and I had a long discussion of the matter one rainy Sunday afternoon not long before she died. So I was very cognizant of her wishes."

"Do other people know how easy access is to your wife's body?" Krow asked.

"Everyone at the funeral was probably aware of it. I'm

sure it was odd enough to become quite a topic of conversation."

The chief cleared his throat carefully. "Well, if that's the case, I guess I can't guarantee that the casket wasn't opened."

"Then I think I'd like to have the mortician who prepared her body reexamine everything to make sure it's all in order—if you have no objections."

"I'm no lawyer, but there is a license you have to get to disinter a body."

"I just want to have a mortician make sure that there's been no vandalism."

"And at the same time look for evidence relating to who killed her?" the chief asked.

The look Chastain gave Amanda and Nick was mildly disappointed.

"I asked them to tell me about what happened at the séance. They didn't have any choice," the chief said. "There isn't any reason why you'd wish to conceal that information, is there?"

"No, of course not. But I see this as being a personal matter."

"We didn't think anything that happened last night had to be kept secret from the police," Amanda said.

"No, I suppose not," Martin Chastain agreed, giving her a conciliatory smile.

"And if you really believe that there might be evidence of the murderer's identity in the coffin, then it's a police matter," the chief said. "So I'm sure you'd want us to know about it."

Martin frowned. "If I'd come to you with the message from the séance, would you have taken me seriously?"

"Maybe not," the chief admitted. "But since somebody

else apparently takes it seriously enough to commit an assault, I'm willing to consider it."

"If the mortician and the cemetery agree, do you have any problem with my trying to find out if the medium's message was accurate by having my wife's coffin examined? Who knows how long it will take if I have to go through all the legal red tape."

The chief hooked his fingers in his belt and stared across the room.

"Since you're the next of kin and the coffin may have already been opened, I don't imagine there will be any problem. But let's check with the management of the cemetery. Who was the mortician?"

"Louis Zenko, right here in town."

"Then get Louis to contact the cemetery management. If they have no objections, I guess I don't."

Chastain nodded, then waved a hand in front of his face. "Please forgive my manners. Have a seat," he said, gesturing to the sofas. "This whole séance thing has thrown me for a loop."

"How did the lock on the doors to the mausoleum get broken in the first place?" asked Amanda once they were seated on the plush sofas.

Chastian shook his head sadly. "It was all my fault. I had that mausoleum built more than twenty-five years ago when my first wife died."

"Your first wife is buried in there as well?" asked Amanda.

"Of course."

Although it probably wasn't all that unusual an arrangement, the thought flashed through Amanda's mind that she wouldn't like to spend eternity in a small stone room with her replacement.

"The long and the short of it is," Martin said, "I forgot where I put the key. I hadn't been in the mausoleum since my first wife's funeral. When I searched for the key right after Larissa's death, it was nowhere to be found."

"So you had the doors opened by a locksmith?" the chief asked.

"Exactly. He took out the lock, but apparently it was an older model that's no longer in common use, so a replacement needed to be ordered from the company. By the time the new lock arrived it was the middle of winter, and we agreed to wait until spring to complete the installation. I thought that a chain and padlock would be adequate security." Chastain cleared his throat as if to emphasize the irony. "After all, I really had no reason to believe that anyone would want to break into a tomb."

"There have never been any problems with vandalism in the past?" Krow asked.

"Not that I know about. I assume the cemetery would have informed me if there were. When we buried Larissa, the mausoleum looked just as I remembered it, although I must admit that at the time I wasn't paying much attention."

He tried to continue speaking but his lips trembled. His eyes slowly filled with tears, as he appeared to be remembering that day six months ago. The chief and Krow looked away.

"Do you live here alone?" Amanda asked gently.

"Yes. Mrs. Ames takes care of things during the day, but she has a place of her own."

"Has Mrs. Ames been with you long?"

"Almost twenty-five years. I hired her shortly after my first wife died. I was very busy starting up my company, and I thought someone needed to be home with William. She used to spend much more time here then. There is a small room off the kitchen where she would occasionally spend the night if I was going to be coming home late."

"Did she get along well with Larissa?" Amanda asked.

"Remarkably well. I'd been concerned that they might not hit it off. After all, Mrs. Ames had been accustomed to running the house for a long while, and I thought she might not take kindly to being replaced. But she and Larissa were like mother and daughter. She hasn't been quite the same since Larissa's death. I think that it's rather lonely for her here now."

"Did Mrs. Ames approve of your attempts to contact Larissa through Mrs. Narapov?" Amanda continued.

Martin chuckled. "Not in the least. Harriet is a down-to-earth, hardheaded woman, and she thought this was a lot of nonsense. A silly waste of time at best and a sacrilege at worst. She let me know her opinion in no uncertain terms. We argued about it a few times, then finally just agreed to disagree."

"Does anyone other than the participants know about what happened at the séance last night?" the chief asked.

"Aside from Mrs. Ames, I mentioned it to Ms. Dewitt, my secretary, when I got to work this morning."

"Did you contact anyone last night?"

Chastain shook his head. "As you probably already know from Mr. Krow and Ms. Vickers, after the séance I had an argument with my son, William. He and his wife left shortly after that. I had a drink with Eric Devlin, my financial consultant, then turned in for an early night. Although I'll admit that I didn't sleep all that well because I had Larissa's message on my mind."

"So you didn't go out at all last night?" the chief asked.

"No."

"You didn't call anyone."

The man shook his head.

"Do you believe that the message from Larissa is real?" Amanda asked softly.

Martin paused, not sure how to answer. "As you know, even last night I was already making plans to act on what Mrs. Narapov said and have my wife's casket opened. But to be completely honest with you, I'm not sure whether I believe the message or not. I have no experience with this kind of thing." He gave a small smile. "I'm an engineer, after all, and so I'm more accustomed to dealing with this world than the next. But I'm willing to venture into areas that I know nothing about if it will help me to find Larissa's killer. I don't see that I have anything to lose."

"What about your credibility as a businessman? Will seemed to be making that point last night," Krow pointed out.

Chastain's blue eyes flashed. "What the world thinks of me hardly matters at this point in my life. I have a highly successful company and more money than I could ever want. The only thing that matters to me now is discovering who took the one thing away from me that I can never replace."

The chief glanced at Amanda and Nick to see if they had any more questions, then thanked Martin Chastain for his time.

When the three were back in the patrol car heading down the road to the center of town, Amanda, who had been looking out the window, asked, "Is that the cemetery where Larissa is?"

The chief nodded.

"It's only a couple of blocks from the Chastain house. You could probably see it from the living room window."

"What are you thinking?" Nick asked. "That Martin left the house right after Eric went home and began prowling around the mausoleum?"

Amanda shrugged. "Maybe his curiosity got the better of him and he didn't want to wait to go through the legal red tape."

"And would Chastain have been desperate enough to hit that boy over the head so as to avoid discovery?" Krow added doubtfully.

"People do funny things," the chief said. "Maybe the boy just surprised him, and he struck out due to a case of nerves. In a dark cemetery at night that could happen. But I don't see any reason why he'd need to cut the chain. After all, he had the key to the padlock. All he had to do was let himself into the mausoleum. The casket was unlocked and in a plastic case that was easily opened. Something my people should have spotted. Anyway, in ten minutes he could have checked things out and been gone with no one the wiser."

"Okay," Nick agreed. "Let's say it wasn't Martin. Who else has a motive?"

"We know William didn't want his father to pursue the matter," the chief said.

"Are you saying that since he didn't want his father to take the medium's message seriously, that proves Will must have killed his stepmother and thought that something in the coffin would incriminate him?" asked Nick with a raised eyebrow.

The chief sighed as he pulled into the parking lot of the inn.

"I don't know what I'm saying, not yet anyway. But I'm thinking that I've been way too casual about this mausoleum. I had one of my officers put a new padlock and chain on the door, but anybody could cut that off in the blink of an eye. Just in case there is something to this clue in the coffin story, I think I'll call that locksmith and have a real lock installed as soon as possible. I'll get a key from the cemetery management, so we can open the gates at night, and arrange to have an officer drive into the cemetery to check periodically on the building"

"I hope it's not the proverbial story of locking the mausoleum door after the clue's gotten out," Amanda said.

The chief nodded. "You're right. Since the coffin wasn't sealed, we can't tell whether that guy last night has already made off with it. But just in case it's still there, I don't want to be lazy."

Chief Toth dropped them off in front of the door to the inn after thanking them for their help. He said he'd be in touch if he needed their services further.

"Did you know that the word *mausoleum* is derived from a man's name?" Nick asked Amanda, as they walked into the lobby of the inn.

She shook her head, guessing that a mini-lecture was coming.

"Mausolus of Caria in ancient Persia," Nick said. "He built this elaborate tomb for himself that was one of the wonders of the ancient world."

"Do tell, professor," Amanda said with a grin.

"Now here's the quiz. What famous building that people visit today is a mausoleum for a man's wife?"

Amanda frowned, pretending to think hard. "Gee whiz, professor, if I don't get this do I have to come to your office for special help?"

Nick gave her a mock leer. "That's right. For very special help."

"The Taj Mahal," Amanda answered.

Nick snapped his fingers. "Darn, I knew you were too smart to fall into my trap. But will you have lunch with me anyway?"

"Sorry, Nick, I promised to have lunch with Marcie. We have to discuss business."

"How about dinner then?"

Amanda paused. "Okay. I want to find out about your secret life as a consultant on the paranormal with the Portland police."

"Sure, but be warned, it's not nearly as exciting as it sounds. Let's say we meet in the lobby around six-thirty?"

Amanda nodded.

"I think I'll take a walk around bustling West Windham," Nick said, turning back toward the front door. "I saw an interesting bookstore when we drove through town this morning. I'll also scope out the scene for a good restaurant for tonight."

Giving her a quick wave, Nick headed out of the lobby with his usual loping stride.

As she climbed the stairs to her room, Amanda discovered that she was smiling.

Chapter Eight

"So you turned him down just like that?" Amanda asked, her eyes opening wide for an instant.

It wasn't often that Marcie surprised her, especially when it came to matters of romance. *This was a valuable reminder,* she thought, *that people are unpredictable, even those you think you know pretty well.*

"Wouldn't you?" Marcie asked, her self-confidence slipping just a shade.

Amanda sighed and glanced around the small restaurant where they were having lunch.

"Tell me again why you blew him off."

"He's a bully. He was browbeating poor Ben."

"He's in law enforcement. Doesn't that go along with the job? Sometimes you have to coerce people into telling the truth."

"That's not what he was doing," Marcie said firmly. "He

was just being cruel because he enjoyed it. If Kirk was really concerned with discovering the truth, he would have been nicer to Ben in order to gain his confidence. I found out more than Kirk did because I didn't try to frighten Ben."

"That just shows you're smarter."

Marcie smiled slightly, still clearly dissatisfied with Amanda's less than complete agreement with her decision to drop Kirk.

Amanda looked out the window at the handful of passersby. They were two blocks from the inn, and the brief walk through the small downtown of West Windham had been relaxing. It was a lot like Wells, a quiet town that thrived largely on the seasonal tourist traffic. Only here the focus was on the surrounding woods and lakes rather than on the ocean.

The manuscript pages they'd been going over for the last half hour had been put into a pile and pushed aside to make way for her tuna fish sandwich and Marcie's large bowl of homemade vegetable soup, which smelled terrific and was causing Amanda to regret her conservative choice. She glanced at Marcie's troubled face and decided that she had to say more.

"No man is perfect," Amanda said and stopped, knowing that banal remark was less than helpful.

"I *know* that," Marcie said, rolling her eyes. "And believe me, I'm willing to make allowances. But I also know what a man with a mean streak is like. My father was an expert at doing really rotten things but making them sound like they were for your own good."

Amanda nodded. She knew that Marcie's father's favorite form of punishment was to lock his daughter in a dark closet for hours at a time in order to teach her respect.

"So I guess that whenever I catch even a hint of cruelty in a man, I run the other way. That's one thing that I just can't forgive."

Amanda slowly chewed her bite of sandwich. "At least you know your own mind," she said when she was done.

"But it is hard to turn down a cute guy like Kirk. I hope I won't regret it," Marcie said wistfully. "I haven't got them lined up with numbers in their hands like at the deli counter."

Amanda laughed at the image, then became serious. "Look, all I'm saying is that not every guy who has a few rough edges is going to turn out to be like your father."

"Have you decided what to do about Jeff?" Marcie asked.

She instantly regretted encroaching on such a sensitive area, knowing that she was being petty, striking back at Amanda for not being more supportive. She quickly stared down into her soup bowl as if the Lake Opal Monster had suddenly appeared there swimming among the carrots and potatoes.

"No," Amanda replied, then looking over at Marcie's worried face and relenting, she went on. "He's leaving on Monday."

"Do you have to decide by then whether to go with him?"

"I guess the idea was that I would let him know before he left if I was going down to D.C. to join him. I wouldn't have to actually move down there until I arranged for a replacement at the magazine."

"Monday. You don't have much time to make up your mind."

"I realize that," Amanda said shortly.

"Sorry, it's none of my business."

"No, no, it's not your fault. I'm irritated with myself because I don't know what to do."

"I thought you liked Jeff."

"There's a big difference between liking someone and moving in with him. Plus, I'm not sure I want to live with someone until I decide to get married. I don't think that usually works out very well. There's not enough sense of commitment, so people break up over the least little thing. I don't want to find myself all alone in Washington wondering how I ended up there."

"But don't you think that he wants to marry you eventually?"

"He didn't exactly get down on one knee and propose," Amanda said, tapping her editing pencil on the table as if that was the least she expected. "When he suggested that I move to Washington with him, he presented it more along the lines of what a great career opportunity it would be for the two of us. He didn't mention being heartbroken if I didn't go with him. That's not exactly a clear sign of commitment."

"No man is perfect," Marcie said, then stopped with a stricken expression that said she wished she could take those words back.

Amanda laughed. "Point taken."

"Are you sure . . ." Marcie began, then paused.

"Sure about what?"

"I was just wondering if you were sure that you weren't the one who was afraid of making a commitment," Marcie said.

That earned her a cool look.

"None of us really knows ourselves all that well, do we?" Amanda answered.

Not knowing what to say to that, Marcie remained silent.

"Now why don't we talk about the Chastain case," Amanda suggested, moving the manuscript pages back in front of her to show that it was time to get down to business. "We're only going to be here today, so we have to use our time efficiently. I think you should talk to Mrs. Narapov, the medium. Get some general information about how she thinks this communicating with the next world works. Try to get a sense of whether she's a fraud or not. I'm going to talk to the housekeeper, Mrs. Ames. I'd like a better idea of what Larissa Chastain was like. If this does turn into an article, we'll need a couple of paragraphs about the deceased."

"I thought we were just helping the chief of police and that it had nothing to do with the magazine."

"There might be a story here," Amanda said vaguely, carefully reapplying her lipstick. "Remember, the reason I was invited to West Windham was to attend that séance, so any story leading off of that is fair game and that includes the Larissa Chastain murder."

Confusion was evident on Marcie's face. "But we don't work for a newspaper. How are we going write about a current murder case for *Roaming New England*?"

"If it ties in with the séance, we'll find a way to make it fit into the 'Weird Happenings' section. You know: Did the ghost of Larissa Chastain reveal the identify of her murderer? Something like that would work."

Marcie made her face blank. It never paid to disagree with Amanda when she was off on one of her journalistic rampages. Having started her career with the *Boston Globe*, her true love was for journalism rather than for writing entertainment features. And if she got too far out of line with the *Roaming* approach to things, Marcie knew that Greg Sheffield, the managing editor, would rein her in.

Amanda suddenly smiled as if aware of her own tendencies. "Okay, maybe I am going a little bit off the deep end here. But if we're going to stay in town today, we may as well do something interesting."

Marcie frowned. "Why do I have to talk to the medium while you see the housekeeper? I always get the weird ones."

"That's because you appear so trusting that they open up to you."

"I've heard all this before."

"Plus you weren't at the séance, so she might not be quite as suspicious of you."

"Okay, but if her head spins around and she starts levitating out of the chair, I'm gone," Marcie declared.

Amanda nodded. "But try to get a picture first."

Chapter Nine

He stood at the window looking out over West Windham. The building wasn't very high, but then neither was the town that was laid out before him. It appeared so peaceful and un-complicated when seen from above, like one of those bu-colic plastic villages constructed for a model train display. The kind of small town city dwellers yearned for when they talked about returning to a quieter, more wholesome way of life.

But to him it had become a nightmare. A stage set for a play where the ending would be his tragic destruction. Every stately tree, every meandering road, every clapboard house seemed to be part of a maze designed solely to entrap him. Ever since that medium's message, he had become convinced that some force either from this world or the next was determined to destroy him.

Was this some bizarre form of self-punishment? Could it

be his own guilt that was doing this to him? Had some part of his own subconscious taken vocal form and shouted out that they should look in the coffin? But he dismissed the idea as soon as it came to mind. He'd never felt guilty about Larissa. Indeed, he missed her as he'd never missed anyone in his life. How could Larissa, if it really was her, be doing this to him? As a ghost she must know how he felt. He frowned. Never having had much time for the supernatural, he realized that his willingness to even think this way was a sign of how rattled he was.

He'd almost killed that boy the other night. And even that had seemed to be part of a plot against him. Just as he was about to open poor Larissa's coffin, he'd heard the footsteps. An instant later and the boy would have seen his face, and he'd have had to kill him. The thought made him shiver. Had it really come to this? A good thing he'd had the nippers he'd used to remove the chain. As his anonymous call to the hospital had confirmed, they'd delivered a stunning blow but not enough to be fatal. Otherwise he really would be a murderer. Imagine the voices that would haunt him then.

There was only one way out of this that he could see. He had to get inside the mausoleum again and open the coffin before Martin Chastain got a chance to look inside. If he didn't, it would all be over.

Chapter Ten

Krow was surprised to realize he had thoroughly enjoyed himself as he watched the young woman place the books he had purchased in a bag emblazoned with the store's logo. It had been a long time since he'd browsed around a bookstore just for pleasure, with no particular purpose in mind. Usually he was looking for something related to one of his classes or a book he had seen reviewed in a professional journal and felt that he had to purchase. This time he had been completely whimsical, selecting a biography of Matisse and a recent bestseller that he had chosen based on nothing more than the cover art.

He smiled to himself at this sudden change in his behavior. He knew that he was intense when it came to his work. Some of his colleagues even called it driven. Nick accepted that fact about himself and knew its cause. He came from a family of ambitious people. His father was the head of surgery at a Boston hospital, and his mother a successful attorney. One of his brothers had followed in his father's footsteps and was developing new surgical techniques for skin grafts, while another brother had entered investment banking and received a Christmas bonus that was four times what Nick made in a year.

Choosing to go into psychology had gotten him branded as something of a rebel by his family, who tended to look at the field as lacking the practical value of medicine while offering none of the financial rewards of law or finance. His occasional forays into the paranormal made things even worse. They had earned him stern comments from his father about quasi-science along with a gentle suggestion from his mother that he might want to make an appointment with one of his colleagues in the clinical branch of his discipline. All this did was increase his interest in the paranormal and make him more intent on bringing the critical eye of science to bear on folk tales and superstition.

Nick took the bag from the clerk and walked outside feeling so carefree that he almost began whistling. Like any good psychologist who can't leave well enough alone, he was about to examine more closely the reason for his almost manic mood, which he suspected was due to the ever-elusive Amanda, when he heard someone call his name. Will Chastain was standing by a car parked in front of the store. As soon as he saw Nick stop, he ran up to him.

"I need to talk to you," he said.

Nick studied his friend's face, trying to read his emotions. Was Will angry with him for helping the police? He could understand how his friend, who had asked him to the séance in the first place, might feel betrayed. But what he saw was more worry than anger.

"I haven't had lunch yet. There's a small place two doors up that looked good if you'd care to join me."

Will nodded. The two men didn't talk until they were seated at a table in the front window of the small restaurant and Nick had ordered a sandwich and soup while Will insisted that he only wanted coffee.

"My father called and said that you were helping the police," Will blurted out as soon as the waitress was out of earshot.

"They asked me for my professional advice because the paranormal was involved," Krow answered.

Will cracked the knuckles of his long fingers and looked down at the scarred surface of the wooden table. "Can you help me too, or would that be a conflict of interest?"

"I'm not being paid, and I'm not even sure that the chief will call on me again. So as long as what you want me to do is legal, I don't see a problem."

"I'm worried about this whole medium thing."

"I gathered last night that you were concerned about the impact that it might have on the company."

"That's only part of it," Will said, waving a hand as if to brush away the company as a trivial concern. "What I'm really worried about is my father's sanity. He's the most down to earth, rational man I've ever known with nothing but contempt for speculation that wasn't grounded in fact. If you couldn't offer evidence to support your opinion, he didn't want to hear about it. I should know. He's always accused me of being the dreamer in the family. Said it showed a lack of character, an unwillingness to face the truth."

Nick watched his friend closely but said nothing.

"Back in college I wanted to be an architect," Will said with a shy smile.

"I didn't know that."

"Yeah, I guess no one did. I kept it to myself. By the end of my freshmen year I'd pretty much decided that engineering really wasn't for me. Oh, I could do the work all right; it just didn't excite me. I'd taken a course in the history of architecture, and I decided that's what I wanted to do. You know how kids are at that age, you pick up a little bit of knowledge about something and suddenly it's the passion of your life."

"What happened?"

"I made the mistake of telling my father."

"He was against it?"

"He said that most architects were just glorified contractors, and if I wanted to do that, there was no need for me to go to college. He'd get me a job hammering nails with some local builder, and I could learn the trade from the bottom up. I tried to tell him about how architecture was more like art, only it was a work of art that enclosed space. He just laughed and said that I didn't have the imagination to be an artist of any kind." Will paused and sighed. "He said that I didn't even have enough imagination to be a good engineer."

"Fathers can sometimes be hard on their sons."

Will rolled his shoulders as if releasing tension. "Yeah. But I thought he might be more understanding. My mother told me once that when he was in college, he got really involved in the drama club. He even thought about becoming an actor."

"Maybe his father said the same thing to him."

"Could be—I never knew my grandfather. Anyway I went back to engineering. I'm not complaining. I've done all right at it. Maybe a little better than my father ever thought I would. My point is that Dad was always aggressively practical. Even though his own inventions have required a lot of imagination, whenever you say that to him, he gets angry and claims that it's all just simple problem solving. That's why it disturbs me so much to see him getting so heavily into the supernatural. It goes against his whole personality."

"If it's any consolation, the impression I got from your father this morning is that he's approaching this paranormal business from a rather scientific perspective. He wants to find out who murdered Larissa, and he's willing, somewhat reluctantly, to use methods that are certainly unorthodox. But I don't think that he automatically accepts what Mrs. Narapov claims to report from the other side. He's keeping an open mind and waiting to see where the facts lead. There's nothing irrational or insane in that."

"He may give the impression of being rational, but he never really has been when it comes to Larissa," William insisted. The waitress brought their orders, and William quickly put two creams in his coffee and began stirring it vigorously, rattling his spoon around the inside of the thick mug. "Larissa has always been his one area of complete blindness."

Nick leaned back in his chair and let his gaze shift to the street. The sky was a vivid blue and the sun warm, but the winds were blustery enough to require a warm coat. He watched a woman with two small children struggle to keep them in tow. He reminded himself that Will's opinion of Larissa was no doubt colored by a lot of emotion.

"I take it that you're basing your opinion on more than the events of last night. The séance alone isn't the first time that your father has been irrational with regard to his wife?"

Will paused as if unsure whether he wanted to continue. Finally he put his hands flat on the table as if about to engage in some form of isometric exercise.

"Look, all I'm saying is that Larissa wasn't as perfect as my father likes to think she was." He paused as if deciding whether to go on. "She had an affair within six months of their marriage."

"With whom?"

"The golf pro at the country club." Will gave an embarrassed smile. "I know it's a cliché, but that doesn't surprise me at all. In my opinion Larissa was sadly lacking in class in the first place."

"Did your father know about this?"

"Eventually, he found out about it. Stories went around the club that the pro was giving Larissa more than just golf lessons, and eventually my father caught wind of it. He confronted the man who was spreading the story and they almost came to blows. The golf pro, of course, denied it when challenged. He convinced my father that it was just the kind of malicious rumor that starts whenever an attractive woman spends a lot of time with a handsome man. My father was more than happy to accept that version of the events. He insisted that Larissa was simply a woman who was relaxed and friendly around men and people misinterpreted her behavior."

"What do you think?"

"I think Larissa was a conniving gold digger who didn't know the meaning of the word *faithful*," Will burst out, his usually placid face reddening with anger.

"Do you have any evidence that she actually was having this affair?"

"Only that where there's smoke there's fire. I couldn't very well dig into it without embarrassing my father."

"So you don't actually know that your father was wrong?"

William shook his head. "But you never met the woman. Sexuality exuded from every pore and whenever she was around an attractive man everything she said was flirtatious. It was obvious to everyone."

Krow wondered if it had been particularly obvious to Will because he was attracted to her. It wouldn't be the first time that a man had universalized his feelings for a woman.

"But not to your father?"

"He had a blind spot when it came to her. He was completely convinced that she loved him and all of her attentions to other men were just harmless fun. I warned Larissa that this couldn't go on forever. That the day would come when she'd do something that even my father wouldn't be able to ignore."

"And what did Larissa say?" Nick asked.

"She laughed at me. She told me that I wasn't half the man my father was and that was why I couldn't understand why ultimately she would be faithful to him."

"What did she mean by 'ultimately'?"

"I took it to mean that she wasn't about to leave him for anyone else. Of course why would she, he was her meal ticket."

"Did you try to discuss it with your father?"

William shook his head.

"Why not?"

"Because I knew he'd just get angry with me. My father

and I are never on what you could call good terms, and if I criticized Larissa to him, he would just suspect that I was jealous of her. That I was angry because she had gotten closer to him than I ever would."

"The chief of police also mentioned something about your inheritance."

"Yeah, the Portland police tried to make a lot out of that. If Larissa had a baby, then it's possible my inheritance would have been divided. But I make a good salary, and my portion of any inheritance would still be enough to leave my family extremely well off."

"Some people can never have enough," Nick pointed out.

"And do you think I'm one of those people?" Will asked bluntly.

Nick stared at him for a moment, then he smiled. "No. I've known you for a long time. If you did resent Larissa, it was because she had your father's affection, not because she might get his money."

"Thank you. And you're right. I *was* jealous of the way she managed to worm her way into his heart. But I wouldn't have killed her, if for no other reason than I knew how much it would have hurt my father."

Nick nodded. He finished the last of his coffee and picked up the check. Will reached for it.

"No, this is on me," Nick said. "All you had was coffee."

"But you did the heavy listening."

"My pleasure. After all, we've been friends for a long time."

"That's why I was hoping there was something you could do for me if your commitment to Chief Toth wouldn't get in the way."

"How can I help?"

"My father just called me. He's gotten permission from the cemetery to have Larissa's coffin removed and taken to the mortuary so it can be checked for damage. At least that's the excuse he's giving."

"But he really wants to see if there's a clue inside that points to her murderer."

Will nodded. "I don't want to be involved. I know my father doesn't really want me there, and I'm not sure that I can stand by and not say something critical. But I was hoping that maybe you would be willing to be present to see if anything important is actually found. I know you won't be dazzled by a lot of supernatural double-talk. I've already asked my father if you could attend, and he's agreed to it."

"Is it really necessary? I'm sure the chief of police will make a point of being present. He strikes me as a smart, sensible person."

"But I want someone there whom I know and trust."

The distress on his friend's face was so clear that Nick figured he couldn't refuse.

"On one condition," he said.

"What?"

"That I can take Amanda Vickers along with me."

"My father said the more the merrier, so I'm sure he wouldn't have a problem with her being there," Will said. Then he gave Nick a sly grin. "But I wouldn't have thought that an exhumation was any woman's idea of a hot date."

Nick arched an eyebrow. "I suppose that all depends on the woman."

Chapter Eleven

Marcie sat in the large, side lobby of the West Windham Inn and realized that she was nervous. She practiced clenching and unclenching her hands. A hockey coach had once suggested that as a way to relieve tension. After Marcie had done that enough to worry that soon her hands would be too tired to write, she glanced around the room taking in the dark furnishings, which only added to its somber mustiness.

Along one wall was a nineteenth-century piano that the helpful desk clerk told her had fewer keys than today's models. In the center of the room was a horsehair sofa, the very idea of which Marcie found somewhat creepy. A selection of upholstered chairs whose tapestry prints were so worn that they no longer told a clear story were positioned around the room in what the staff must have thought were potential conversational groupings. These were intermixed with dark mahogany tables, black and sticky with old varnish, that held heavily shaded lamps.

Marcie had eventually perched on the newest looking chair in the room, which fortunately was within speaking distance of another, so that the arrangement would work for her interview with Mrs. Narapov. Although Marcie had met with a number of people over the last couple of months who claimed to have had extraordinary experiences, this would be her first contact with someone who contacted the dead on a professional basis. The thought of someone talking to the dead as a profession made her want to giggle nervously. She suppressed the desire quickly as a woman wearing a large cape over a housedress and sporting sensible crepe-soled shoes entered the room and headed in her direction.

"Ms. Ducasse, I presume," the woman said in a carefully controlled voice.

Marcie stood up and shook the woman's hand, feeling like a schoolgirl.

When they were both seated, Mrs. Narapov looked hard at Marcie and said, "I only agreed to meet with you because you are helping the chief of police with his investigations. I am not interested in having an article written about me in your magazine, and I would appreciate it, if you should write anything about the Larissa Chastain case, that my name not be mentioned."

"That can certainly be arranged, if it's what you wish."

"I do."

Marcie opened her notebook, where she had jotted down a few questions, and took out a pen.

"I was wondering if you could give me a bit of background information on the history of mediums."

Mrs. Narapov stared at her. "There are a number of standard histories on the subject which can give you that information."

Marcie's pen stayed poised in midair. She had already learned in her brief stint on the magazine that by not accepting a person's first answer you often got more. Her expectant expression eventually wore the woman down.

"The standard histories begin with Maggie and Katie Fox who in 1849 in Hydesville, New York, began communicating with spirits in their house by means of rapping on the walls. A few years later, the Davenport brothers toured extensively using a box in which they claimed to communicate with spirits. The second half of the nineteenth century was rich with mediums who contacted those who had crossed over."

"Is that when ectoplasmic manifestations began?"

The woman nodded. "Rightly or wrongly, some mediums insisted that the spirits they contacted take a physical form."

"Do you do that?"

Mrs. Narapov sighed, as if wearied by the public ignorance that surrounded her.

"I could if I wished, but I don't believe in asking spirits to take on a material form because it is often very distressing to them. Would you want to put old dirty clothes onto a new, clean body?"

That depends on how much trouble it is to do the laundry, Marcie thought, but decided that would be too flippant to say.

"And you contact the spirits through a guide or a control?"

"When I am doing a full séance, I have a control that I use, but often the spirits speak to me directly, especially if they have something pressing to say to a loved one who has been left behind."

"Are the messages you receive always accurate?"

The woman smiled complacently. "That depends on how you define *accuracy*. Are any of our senses always accurate? Sometimes the messages are open to interpretation and as mere humans we may misunderstand. The next world is very different from this one, and it is difficult for the spirits to remember how to communicate on this plane. They must often employ symbols."

"How did you come to meet Martin Chastain?"

"We were introduced by mutual friends in Boston. They knew how troubled Martin was by the death of his wife and thought that I might possibly provide him with some comfort."

"By enabling him to contact his dead wife?"

The woman nodded. "Sometimes when things are left unsaid, it is difficult for both the dead and those that survive them to rest. In this case, Martin was clearly anxious to discover who had murdered his wife, and it is quite possible that Larissa was causing this anxiety."

"She wanted her murderer discovered, so she was haunting Martin?"

"Put crudely. Haunting is such an imprecise word. I'd rather say that she was disturbing his rest by gently goading him to action. Spirits in most cases cannot actually control us, but they can inspire us to act in certain ways."

"I see." Marcie chewed on the end of her pen. "I guess I would have thought that the dead sort of get on with it in the next world rather than worrying about finding justice in this one."

"Each spirit is an individual, just as they were in life," the medium answered.

"So you think Larissa is out for justice."

"Definitely."

"Then we should find something in the coffin that will give us a clue to her murderer."

The medium's expression showed a trace of doubt. "As I said, these things are open to interpretation."

It was Marcie's turn to smile. "I wouldn't think there was much room for interpretation here. Either there's something in the coffin or there isn't."

Mrs. Narapov's expression suddenly went slack and her eyes closed. Marcie feared she was witnessing a stroke and was about to ask the woman if she was all right when her eyes opened suddenly and bored into Marcie's. "Is there someone from your family that has crossed over recently?"

Marcie wanted to stand up, walk across the lobby, and return to her room where she would carefully type up her notes. She could even picture herself doing each of these things precisely in that order. But she stayed seated in the chair in the dimly lit parlor, staring into Mrs. Narapov's eyes. Her arms were too heavy to move from her lap, and her legs had suddenly broken free of any connection to her mind.

"Why do you ask?" she managed to ask.

"Because there is a spirit calling to me that wishes to tell you something. Do you know who that could be?"

Marcie knew that it had to be her mother who had died a year ago. Who else could it be? Her mother who had never stopped her father from locking her in dark places when she was a child. Her mother who had dismissed all that he had done with a shrug and the comment that he was a good husband and father so they had to ignore his "little ways."

"I know who it is," Marcie said angrily. "What does she want to tell me?"

Mrs. Narapov frowned as if struggling to hear a far off voice echoing over a vast distance and across the chasm between dimensions.

"She says . . . she says that she's sorry."

Darkness descended. Marcie felt herself falling into a pit so black that she couldn't tell if she was going up or down. All of her senses had disappeared. She blinked frantically and slowly the darkness passed. She was staring down at the worn carpet. Not sure how much time had gone by, Marcie summoned her courage and glanced up. Mrs. Narapov looking at her with a satisfied smile.

"Is there anything else that you need to ask me?"

Marcie shook her head and mumbled, "Thank you for your time."

Pulling her cape around her, the medium walked across the room with the careful tread of someone who spent much of her life traversing an unsettled world.

Chapter Twelve

Amanda knocked on the front door of the Chastain house. Having walked up from the inn, she was feeling cold and windblown by the time she arrived and was hoping that Mrs. Ames would let her in promptly. When she had called an hour before, she had carefully explained to Mrs. Ames that she wanted to find out what kind of a woman Larissa Chastain had been, and she had promised to not ask any questions about the murder. It had been difficult to convince the woman that her primary concern was with seeing that Larissa was properly depicted if any story about the séance were to be written. Finally, the housekeeper had agreed, although Amanda could tell that the first time she stepped over the line Mrs. Ames would happily show her the door.

Mrs. Ames immediately appeared on the doorstep and held the door open wide for her to enter. Amanda hung her coat on one of the brass hooks of an antique coat tree that stood to her right in the hallway. She was disappointed there wasn't an elephant's leg umbrella holder. That would have fit in beautifully with the decor.

"We'll talk in the kitchen," the woman announced.

Without saying another word, the housekeeper led the way down the main hall toward the back of the house and Amanda followed. The hallway became narrower behind the stairway and eventually led into the kitchen. If she'd had to guess what the kitchen would be like before seeing it, Amanda would have described a typical early twentieth-century kitchen: dark stained cabinets reaching up to eleven-foot ceilings, old white appliances, and walls of institutional green with a heavily used wooden table holding pride of place in the center of the room. Instead what she found was a bright, cheerful kitchen with a bay window looking out on the back lawn, granite countertops everywhere, a two-level island with stools, and commercial-grade stainless steel appliances. In short, it was a contemporary dream kitchen.

"Would you like a cup of coffee?" the housekeeper asked.

"Yes, please," Amanda said, hopping up on one of the stools at the granite island.

She watched while Mrs. Ames drew a cup of coffee from yet another complicated stainless steel mechanism that looked to be professional grade. Her surprise must have been evident on her face because Mrs. Ames smiled slightly as she handed her the coffee and slid over a plate of homemade cookies that Amanda suspected would add inches by just looking at them.

"The room isn't what you expected?"

"Much more modern."

The woman nodded and sat on a stool across the island from Amanda.

"This is all Larissa's influence. She said that no one should have to cook in a kitchen that's out of date. Mr. Chastain's first wife, William's mother, selected this house. I never met her, but from all accounts she was a bit of a fanatic when it came to historical accuracy. Everything had to either remain unchanged or be restored to what it was like when the house was first built. Granted, she did allow the kitchen appliances to be updated to when she first moved into the house in the late sixties, but there were no changes after that."

"Historical restorations are popular today, but I don't think it was all that fashionable back then."

"It wasn't. But the first Mrs. Chastain had studied history at Mount Holyoke College and fancied herself something of a historian. She was very much taken with the idea of living in the past."

"But Larissa wasn't?"

A brief smile flitted across her face. "Oh my, no. She thought the whole house was unbelievably dreary. If she had lived, every room would eventually have been redecorated."

"How long was Larissa married to Mr. Chastain?"

"It would have been two years last month." The woman paused and looked across the kitchen. Amanda could see that she was fighting back her emotions. Apparently Martin Chastain had been correct in saying that Mrs. Ames and Larissa had something of a mother-daughter relationship.

"But this was the only room she had remodeled in those two years?"

"Mr. Chastain isn't a man to handle change well, especially in his domestic life. From what I've heard, he can be quite innovative when it comes to his work, but he likes things at home to be predictable. Larissa was slowly working on him, and she did get him to allow her to renovate their bedroom last fall. They took down walls and added dual walk-in closets and a large dressing room off of the master bath. I'll show it to you later."

"From all accounts Larissa was a very active, vibrant woman. Did she have much to do with the running of the house?"

"It took a little while for us to come to an understanding," Mrs. Ames admitted. "I think Larissa would have been happy to take over the entire running of the house, at least on a managerial level. She wouldn't have been interested in actually cooking or cleaning herself, but planning the menu and controlling the household accounts would have appealed to her. But I made it quite clear from the beginning that those were my duties. After a brief period of adjustment, she understood that, and from then on we got along very well."

So Larissa was smart enough to know when she couldn't win a battle, and had managed to turn a potential enemy into an ally, Amanda thought, which indicated that if she was a gold digger, she certainly wasn't a simple-minded one.

"If Larissa didn't run the house, then how did she spend her time?"

"Mr. Chastain is an important member of the community, but his business takes up so much of his energy that many of the local civic activities expected of him are done by Will. After Martin and Larissa married, she took over some of those responsibilities. Will is on the library board and a trustee of an area college. Larissa helped plan the hospital ball and organized benefits for local charities. She was also a volunteer at the art museum in Portland and raised money for the symphony. Those activities kept her rather busy."

Amanda wondered whether William and Larissa's paths had crossed often, and if that led to conflict, or perhaps the growth of something else.

"Does Will live in West Windham as well?"

Mrs. Ames nodded. "About a mile from here."

"Does he get along with his father?" Amanda asked.

Mrs. Ames took so long to answer that Amanda feared that she had crossed the line and was going to be asked to leave. But when the housekeeper began to speak, there was a softness of fond recollection on her face.

"When I first came here Will's mother had just died, and the poor boy was so alone. He'd wander around the house looking in every room like he expected to find his mother hiding somewhere. My heart went out to him."

"How old was he?"

"Ten. He'd been very close to his mother, and it was difficult for him after she died. That's not to say that Mr. Chastain wasn't a good father. He made a point of talking to the boy when he was home, but he's not by nature an outgoing man. And that was when his business was beginning to really take off, so he was hardly ever home. But you should have seen the boy's face when his father walked in the door. He idolized his father and would have done anything to please him."

"What about as he got older?" asked Amanda.

The housekeeper shrugged at the obviousness of it all.

"He became an engineer didn't he? Just like his father." She lowered her voice. "Sometimes I think that he married Bethany because she was the first of his girlfriends that his father liked. But none of that helped, Mr. Chastain is a man who admires brilliance, and that's one thing that William will never have. He's a sweet, smart, gentle man, but he'll never have the genius of his father."

Amanda paused and took a sip of coffee. Her heart went out to William, who must have heard this sentiment expressed or at least implied all his life.

"But Larissa probably wasn't a genius either."

The harsh bark of laughter from Mrs. Ames startled her. "What man judges a woman the same way he judges a man? What Martin loved about Larissa was her youth and enthusiasm, the excitement she brought into his life. I think it was the first time he'd really known a woman like that, and he couldn't believe that she was interested in him. Plus she was as different from the first Mrs. Chastain as chalk from cheese. She made him feel young again."

"And how did William feel about all of this?"

"When I looked over at him during their wedding, I saw the same hurt look on his face as when his mother died. I think he'd felt that now he'd lost his other parent."

"So they didn't get along?"

Mrs. Ames snatched away Amanda's half-full coffee cup and put it over by the sink, letting her know that she'd gone too far.

"I don't have all day. Let's go upstairs. I'll show you Larissa's bedroom."

Amanda followed the woman out into the main hallway

and up the wooden staircase with its intricately carved spindles and wide banister, the restoration of which had probably been one of the projects of the first Mrs. Chastain. Amanda could well imagine how it must have bothered Larissa to be living in this museum that had been created by her predecessor.

At the top of the stairs, they turned to the right and went down to the end of the hall where Mrs. Ames, with a surprisingly theatrical flourish, opened a set of double wooden doors. The dramatic entrance proved to be well deserved as Amanda entered a room that was larger than her entire apartment. Light flooded the corner room from two sides, and at one end on a raised platform stood a large canopy bed looking like it would be appropriate for a member of royalty. A sitting area had been established by one of the front windows and was separated off from the rest of the room by a faded but no doubt authentically expensive Persian rug. Mrs. Ames pushed a small button on the headboard of the bed and from a large chest across the room a television arose as if by magic.

"Larissa loved that. She'd play with it over and over again and laugh," Mrs. Ames said.

The housekeeper led Amanda across the room into a large dressing room. One wall was filled with what appeared to be custom-made cabinetry. Mrs. Ames pulled open a series of drawers and revealed a treasure trove of jewelry. Amanda drew closer to examine it.

"None of it is very expensive," said the housekeeper with a smile. "Larissa said that she couldn't tell a diamond from zirconium, and she doubted that most other people could either. But she liked to wear bright, shimmering things."

Amanda noticed that the jewelry seemed to be arranged in pairs. As she looked closer it became clear that many of the pieces had been purchased in duplicate.

When she mentioned this, Mrs. Ames chuckled. "Larissa used to joke about that fact that she was a chronic loser, always misplacing things and often not finding them again for weeks. So whenever she come on a piece of jewelry she liked, if it wasn't very expensive, she'd buy a backup."

Amanda marveled at the rows of bracelets, necklaces, pins, and rings neatly displayed on velvet trays as if in a jewelry store window. Many of them nestled next to an identical twin.

"All of this is costume stuff, of course. She only had a few valuable pieces, and those were kept in a locked jewelry cabinet." Mrs. Ames gestured to a drawer with a shiny brass lock. "The only jewelry she wore all the time were her wedding ring and a jade locket with a picture of herself and Mr. Chastain."

"Did she have duplicates of them?"

Mrs. Ames shook her head. "Not of her wedding ring. She used to joke that multiple wedding rings might show a lack of commitment. But she did have another locket. The lockets aren't here. One was misplaced just before she died and hasn't turned up yet."

"And the other?" Amanda finally asked when the woman didn't go on.

Mrs. Ames sighed. "Martin put it around her neck just before they closed the casket."

"So she wasn't wearing one on the day she died, or else the police would have held on to it as evidence."

Mrs. Ames nodded slowly. "Just before she went out the

door that day Larissa said that she couldn't find either one of her lockets. She laughed and said that maybe she should get three of them, but I could tell that it bothered her to be without it. I guess Martin found one of them before the funeral."

"Did she have much opportunity to wear all of these things? I may be wrong, but Martin Chastain didn't impress me as the kind of man who would have an extensive social life."

Mrs. Ames laughed. "That's an understatement. He lives for his work, always has. The only events he goes to are conferences and banquets that are directly related to the business. Larissa would attend some of them as well or at least she would go to the social activities. But as I said, she had an active social life of her own based on her charity work. Her involvement in the museum, the symphony, and various charities meant she had lots of invitations to parties, gallery openings, and honors banquets."

"Did she go alone?"

"Sometimes." Mrs. Ames paused as if determining how much information she should volunteer. "Like I told you before, Larissa and Will used to handle most of the charity work, so sometimes they'd go to things together."

"Even though they didn't get along?"

"I never said that," Mrs. Ames snapped, then she went on more calmly, "William realized that being the public face of Chastain Industries was part of his job. Larissa knew she had certain duties as Martin's wife, plus she enjoyed meeting new people. They probably didn't spend much time together once they arrived at an event."

Mrs. Ames went down the other side of the dressing room,

sliding back multiple doors to reveal yards of clothing neatly arranged on rods set at varying heights. Outside of a clothing store, Amanda had never seen such a display. If she had owned even half this much, she'd never get out the door in the morning because of the number of decisions that would have to be made.

"Did Larissa actually wear all of these things?"

"Oh, yes. She had a rule: anything she hadn't worn in a year she gave away. She didn't believe in hoarding clothes. 'Clothes should belong to the people who want to wear them,' she would say."

"Larissa must have been a very decisive woman," Amanda said, running her hand along a row of silk blouses, enjoying the sensation.

"She was," Mrs. Ames said. She closed the doors and led Amanda out into the hall to show that the tour was over. "But she also enjoyed dressing up, almost like a little girl. Each day she'd try to pick an outfit to match her mood."

Or to make a certain impression on people, Amanda thought, as she followed the housekeeper down the stairs and returned to the front hall. Larissa must have been quite the actress. Amanda put on her coat and turned to the woman.

"Thank you for all your help," she said, putting out her hand.

Mrs. Ames gave it a brief, businesslike shake.

"I didn't let you ask me any questions about that murder because I really know nothing about it," she said quickly, as if suddenly deciding that Amanda deserved some sort of explanation. "Larissa left for Portland that afternoon to go shopping, and as I've told the police, she seemed the same as usual. And although I think all of this ghost business is just so much silliness, I can understand why Mr. Chastain is doing it. Nothing will be the same here until we know what happened to Larissa."

"I can understand that," Amanda replied.

As she walked back to the inn, Amanda walked along the fence that defined the boundaries of the cemetery and found her eyes repeatedly being drawn along the irregular rows of tombstones as she wondered exactly which of the small stone buildings held Larissa Chastain's body.

Chapter Thirteen

Marcie sat in the mahogany rocking chair that occupied one corner of her room, gently moving back and forth. The motion was soothing to her, and she had been sitting there since returning from her interview with Mrs. Narapov. She felt as if her mind were slowly coming out from under the influence of a powerful drug. Her thoughts had gradually begun to clear, but the emotional shock of the medium's message was still very real. How had Mrs. Narapov known precisely the sort of thing that her mother would say to her if she could? Always apologizing, but never dealing with the problem. A flash of anger made Marcie's stomach clench. She wasn't past her rage even now that her mother was dead. But did the rightness of the message mean that Mrs. Narapov really was able to contact the next world? Her thoughts started to spin again in an unsettling way.

As usual, when ideas were disturbing her, Marcie decided that moving her body would be the best solution. A little exercise always helped to clear her mind. She threw on her coat and headed downstairs. Just as she reached the lobby, Nick Krow came in the front door. He immediately recognized her from their brief meeting the previous afternoon and smiled.

"Just heading out?"

Marcie forced herself to sound normal. "Yeah. I thought I'd take a quick walk around old West Windham."

"I was hoping to get a chance sometime to hear about your research on the Monster of Lake Opal. I like to keep a record of these stories for my own files."

A debate took place in Marcie's mind between the relative advantages of clearing her head by means of a walk versus a conversation with a handsome man.

"The walk can wait," she said firmly. "I'd like a chance to discuss what I've managed to find out."

"Shall we talk in there?" Nick asked, pointing to the side room where she'd had her conversation with Mrs. Narapov a short time ago.

Marcie paused for an instant, then charged ahead into the dimly lit room, hoping that a conversation with Nick would help disperse whatever bad vibrations the room held for her. But she made a point of making a beeline to a different seating area than the one she'd shared with Mrs. Narapov. No sense in overly tempting fate.

"So why don't you tell me about the Monster of Lake Opal?" Nick said, once they were settled in two worn chairs.

After taking a deep breath to compose her thoughts,

Marcie gave a careful summary of her research, ending with a humorous description of her tour around Lake Opal with Kirk and Ben. When she was done, she sat back and smiled. Although Nick was a college professor and that should have made her a bit nervous, his friendly attitude and willingness to laugh at her jokes had put her at ease.

"It sounds like you've done a thorough job of checking out this Ben Hanson's story. In fact, with all of the time and research you've put into the folklore behind this monster, you probably deserve more credit for the article than he does."

Marcie shook her head. "I'd never have heard about it except for him. It's his story. It's unique."

"I don't want to disillusion you," Nick said slowly, "but actually there are quite a few stories about creatures of this sort."

"Really?"

Marcie's face fell so dramatically that Nick had to smile.

"I'm afraid so. In fact I can think of at least three from this general area right off the top of my head. There's the Silver Lake Serpent in Wyoming County, New York, that goes back to the middle of the nineteenth century, although some people think that's been proven to be a hoax. Then there's the Lake Utopia Monster from up in New Brunswick, Canada. But the one that's been researched the most is Champ."

"Champ?" Marcie asked, giggling at the name.

"Because he purportedly lives in Lake Champlain. Just like with your monster, there are reports of sightings going back to the late nineteenth century. In fact some even claim that Samuel de Champlain himself saw the creature back in 1609, but that's questionable. There's a purported photo of Champ that people have been arguing about for over twenty years. Plus there's been lots of scientific research by cryptozoologists."

"You mean there are guys who specialize in checking out mysterious creatures?"

"That's right. They've gone out there with sonar and remote underwater vehicles to try to get the proof. So far it's all been pretty inconclusive."

Marcie leaned forward in her chair, her eyes wide with excitement.

"But do you think it's possible?"

Nick shrugged noncommittally. "I suppose it's possible, especially in Lake Champlain. That's a large body of water, and you'd need lots of water for a herd of creatures large enough to stay in existence for several hundred years. The real question is whether there are more probable explanations for all these so-called sightings."

"Kirk said that most people think the Monster of Lake Opal is just a floating log."

"That's always a possibility. But anything that swims could be the culprit: salmon, sturgeon, schools of small fish, muskrats, beavers, otters—the list of alternative explanations is pretty long."

"But none of those sound like a creature with a long neck sticking out of the water," Marcie objected.

Nick smiled. "Of course, you have to take into account that people do exaggerate things, especially when they've heard about a monster and are expecting it."

Marcie sank back into her chair, disappointed.

"And the other issue is, why haven't all these researchers been able to find the remains of a Champ-like creature. They've been searching the lake bottom with various devices for some time, but so far no luck. Of course, it would take some luck to find the carcass of anything on the bottom of a lake that large."

"So it's still a possibility?"

Nick held up his hands in mock defeat. "But I wouldn't go so far as to say a probability."

"And what about my monster in Lake Opal?"

"A much smaller lake, so less likely. Of course, it is rather close to Sebago Lake. They could be connected by an underground river of some sort and that would greatly increase the breeding area." Nick shrugged. "But I think you'd better just be happy with having a good story. You could spend twenty years and millions of dollars and still not have any more useful evidence than you have now."

"Yeah, I guess so. It's just frustrating not knowing."

"When it comes to the supernatural, you're always dealing with something less than certainty. You always have to balance possibility against probability."

"'I didn't expect to find the two of you here," Amanda said, coming into the room. "Am I disturbing anything?"

She was a bit surprised to find Nick and Marcie chatting together like old friends. Nick had one leg crossed over the other at the knee in the casual way that for some reason reminded Amanda of men lounging in Parisian cafés reading the newspaper and sipping milky coffee. It made him look even more attractive than usual.

"Nick and I were just comparing notes on monsters," Marcie said as Amanda settled gracefully onto an ornate footstool.

Amanda nodded and considered whether to tell Nick about her visit to Mrs. Ames. As a reporter she had developed a tendency to keep her research confidential, but since the three of them were working as a team on the Chastain case, she decided that it was only right to be open with him. When she had completed a brief summary of what she had learned, Nick shook his head.

"It doesn't really bring us any closer to a suspect, does it?"

"But it does help us to develop a clearer idea of what Larissa Chastain was like. She was a clever woman who knew how to get her way with people. The proof of it is that she was even able to get on the good side of Mrs. Ames."

"She also sounds like someone who wouldn't have cared to share Martin's reclusive lifestyle. Her involvement in all those social activities proves that," Nick said.

"Some of which she went to with Will. I wonder what their relationship was actually like."

"Not the most congenial, if you believe Will," Nick began, and he went on to relate Will's story about Larissa's affair with the golf pro.

"And Martin didn't believe the gossip?" Amanda asked.

"Not according to Will. He seems to feel that his father was virtually bewitched by her."

"Speaking of witches," Amanda said, turning to Marcie. "What did you learn from Mrs. Narapov?"

Marcie shook her head. "Nothing much. A little about the history of mediumship, I guess you'd call it. She's not the most outgoing person in the world."

Marcie wanted to talk about her experience with Narapov, but she didn't care to appear weak or stupid in front of Nick. There'd be time enough later to discuss the matter alone with Amanda.

"Well, I guess you're right," Amanda concluded. "We really haven't gotten anywhere much except to discover that Larissa might have been unfaithful."

"And that Martin was besotted with her, and Will was jealous of her closeness to his father," Nick concluded.

"I guess that's it, then," Amanda said with a note of finality. "We go home. We can ask the chief to get in touch with us if the case is ever solved."

Nick cleared his throat. "Actually we've been invited to an exhumation tomorrow."

"*We* have?" Amanda's eyes narrowed questioningly.

"Martin has gotten permission to open Larissa's coffin, and Will would like me to be there to represent him. I figured that you'd want to come along."

"You did?"

"I'm sure that you saw some pretty bad things when you were a reporter in Boston. There must have been dead bodies once in a while."

Amanda nodded bleakly. "But not dead for six months."

Nick smiled. "At least there's no blood."

"Since this all started with Mrs. Narapov's message about a clue in the coffin, examining the body would kind of give us closure," Marcie said.

Amanda glanced at her friend to see if she was making a sick joke: *closure as in the lid of a coffin coming down or in this case coming up,* Amanda thought grimly. But at least it would give her another day away from her real life, the one in which she had to make a decision about Jeff.

"Okay, okay, I'll call Greg. If he can spare us for another day, we'll stay through tomorrow."

"There's another thing," Nick said.

Amanda rolled her eyes.

"I know that I promised to take you out to dinner tonight, but how would you like to go on a camping trip instead?" he asked with a sheepish grin.

"Camping in Maine in the middle of March. That sounds like fun only for a masochist," Amanda replied.

"I'm not talking about recreational camping," Nick said. "What I'm planning is more in the nature of guarding evidence."

"And exactly what evidence would that be?"

"Well, I was hoping that we could keep an eye on the Chastain mausoleum tonight just in case someone decided to make a second attempt at breaking into the coffin."

"Aren't the police already doing that?" Amanda asked.

"At the most they're only going to stop by a couple of times a night and that depends on the number of calls they have to handle."

"Maybe the three of us could stay at Ben's, and we could take turns out in the cemetery keeping watch on the place," said Marcie. "It might take a bit of talking, but I'll bet Ben would be willing to have us use his place as long as there weren't any police involved."

"This would be Ben, the vampire hunter," Amanda said dryly.

Marcie grinned. "That's probably a gross exaggeration. Let me give him a call."

She pulled her cell phone out of her bag and walked across the room.

"Not that I have any doubt about your physical prowess," Amanda said to Krow, "but are you planning to personally apprehend this intruder yourself if he happens to put in an appearance?"

He shook his head. "If we spot something, we call the police. I'm not trying to catch the guy. I'm just trying to keep him out of the mausoleum. According to Will, the coffin is being removed to the mortuary tomorrow for examination. So it's just tonight that I'm concerned about."

"We really should tell the chief."

"He'd just warn us off." Nick leaned forward, his face etched with concern. "If someone breaks into the coffin tonight, we'll never know if a clue to the murder was there or not. Imagine how we'll feel."

I'll feel like I'd had a good night's sleep, Amanda thought but couldn't say, given the earnest expression on his face. She could sense that he was relishing the opportunity to play the part of a man of action. Something she'd come to suspect in men because it usually led to trouble.

"Any clue could already have been removed by the intruder last night."

"But we don't *know* that."

Amanda sighed resignedly. "We call the police as soon as we see anything out of the ordinary, right? We still don't know what we're tangling with here, and that boy got hit on the head pretty hard last night."

Nick nodded soberly.

"Definitely no heroics," Nick promised, sketching a cross over his heart.

"Okay, I guess I'm in," said Amanda.

"Great!" Marcie shouted, walking back across the room. "I got Ben to let us use his place. This will be fun."

It isn't a pajama party, Amanda wanted to point out, but she decided that there was no point trying to go against the momentum.

Nick got to his feet.

"I'm going out to buy some warmer clothes. I didn't come equipped for that kind of thing. Do either of you need stuff?"

Marcie shook her head. "I brought my parka and gloves. I'm all set."

"I could use something to cover my head," Amanda said. "If you see a hooded sweatshirt, would you pick that up for me?"

"What size?"

"Better get a large. I'll probably be wearing it over a sweater or two," Amanda said with a frown.

Nick smiled. "It won't be that bad. This is late March. The temperature at night probably will stay in the twenties."

"Let's hope so," Amanda said, thinking that the twenties didn't sound exactly balmy.

"Will you be coming back to the inn for dinner?" Marcie asked Nick.

"Nope. I spotted a general store a few blocks away that makes its own sandwiches. I think I'll bring some stuff back and have it in my room after I take a nap."

"Where and when are we going to meet?" Amanda asked.

"How about right here in the lobby around eight-thirty?" Nick answered. "I doubt that anyone is going to try vandalizing a coffin before nine."

"Sounds fine," Amanda replied.

"Should we eat here?" Marcie asked her after Nick left the lobby.

Amanda nodded. "We may as well. Our expense account can handle it, but I think Nick's idea of a nap is a good one. Who knows how much sleep we'll get tonight?" She checked her watch. "How about we meet down here in an hour and a half. That will still give us time to have dinner and be ready for Nick."

"And we can compare notes over dinner?" Marcie asked.

Amanda detected a note of anxiety in Marcie's voice. "Unless there's something you'd like to talk about now."

Marcie shook her head. "It'll wait."

He stood at his window and stared over the tops of the buildings to where the headstones marched in ragged rows, like disorderly soldiers attacking the slopes of the low hillside. He knew that he had to get into the mausoleum tonight. Tomorrow Larissa's body was going to be meticulously examined. He didn't dare hope that the one thing that could ruin his life would go undetected. It was possible, but not likely enough to bet his future on it. He smiled bitterly at the thought that life always seemed to be a matter of calculating odds. If only he could be certain that breaking into the mausoleum was a necessity, he'd be able to devote more enthusiasm to the idea, but the lingering notion that this was all a foolish risk made him uncertain, sapping his strength.

He thought back to when he had seen the object placed in the coffin. There had been a moment of blind panic when it had taken all of his will power not to snatch it out of the coffin and run off before the gaze of the stunned onlookers. Then his sober, rational mind shone like the sunlight through the dark panic, telling him this item would be resting with Larissa for eternity. In fact, he had thought with a mental laugh, there was actually no safer place for it. No one would now be likely to accidentally come upon it while sorting through Larissa's things. The one object that could lead to his ruin would now never be discovered. He had immediately concealed his smile of delight for fear of shocking the others.

All would have remained well, of course, except for that medium. He had dismissed the idea of a séance as the harmless action of a heartbroken old man. However, that so-called message from the beyond threatened to destroy his life. And it wasn't even true—at least not completely. But how could anyone have come even that close to getting things right? It was almost as though Larissa had wanted to reveal a different secret, perhaps one that she herself felt guilty about. He thumped his head hard against the window frame as if the impact would somehow rearrange his thoughts to make sense of what was happening.

Nothing became any clearer. However, the flash of pain made him more certain that he had to act.

Chapter Fourteen

"It was uncanny, don't you think? I mean how could she have known that was just the sort of thing my mother would say?"

Marcie and Amanda were eating an early dinner in the inn's restaurant. Marcie had just recounted her experience with Mrs. Narapov. Now she put down her knife and fork and stared across the table at Amanda with a look that challenged her friend to explain the medium's statement.

Amanda took a slow drink of water to give herself time to formulate a careful answer and to give Marcie a chance to breathe and calm down.

"Let's consider this rationally," Amanda began. "She asked if anyone in your family had died recently. That's a pretty safe question. If you had said no, she'd have probably just nodded her head wisely and said nothing. But the odds are pretty good that if you define *recently* broadly enough, many people have lost some family member in the last few years."

"But how would Narapov know that my mother never stood up for me with Dad, and that she felt guilty about it?"

"She didn't know," Amanda said firmly. " 'I'm sorry' is probably one of the most common phrases in the English language. Even if you couldn't think of an immediate reason why someone who died might be apologizing to you, with a little thought you could probably come up with one."

Marcie still looked skeptical.

"Okay, let's say your Aunt Bessie dies and you get the message "I'm sorry" from her spirit. At first you have no idea what that might mean, but the more you think about it, the more you remember that year when she forgot your birthday or didn't send a Christmas present. Before long you're certain that she must have been talking about that and that the message is right on target. Your mind makes up a story that gives the message plausibility."

Marcie gave that explanation some thought. "Okay, I get that. I guess I was kind of naïve, but why was it so convincing when it happened? I even felt kind of funny, like I really was in the presence of something supernatural."

"Maybe she put you in a mild hypnotic trance. I've heard that some mediums can do that. You were sitting in a dark room and had the idea of paranormal happenings on your mind. You were very open to hypnotic suggestion."

"So now I'm easily hypnotized as well as obviously naïve," Marcie said grumpily.

"You said that all this happened right after you started

pressing Narapov on whether her message could definitely be proven true or not."

Marcie nodded.

"That's interesting."

"Why?"

"Well, maybe she was uncomfortable with your question and was trying to prevent you from pursuing it. She could be unhappy with saying something that can be so clearly contradicted."

"Then why say it in the first place?" Marcie asked.

Amanda forked up some of her salad and chewed thoughtfully.

"I can only think of two reasons. One is that maybe Larissa really did send that message, so Mrs. Narapov had no choice."

Marcie made a snorting sound. "*You* don't believe that. I'm the naïve one."

"The other reason," Amanda went on, "is that she had some ulterior motive for wanting to pass along that message. A motive that was important enough for her to take the risk of being proven wrong."

"What reason could that be?"

Amanda shrugged. "I have no idea."

Marcie cut off a large rectangle of her pot roast and fit it in her mouth, then gave a small moan of pleasure.

"You know this really is tender enough to eat with a spoon," she said, following the meat with a large forkful of mashed potatoes.

Amanda glanced up from her flounder filet, which she was consuming in delicate forkfuls. Marcie looked at her own overloaded fork and decided to change the subject as a form of distraction.

"So why do you think Larissa Chastain bought all those clothes and jewelry?" Marcie asked, amazed.

Amanda was tempted to say that some women liked those things, but she stopped herself from making what might sound like an implied criticism of her assistant, whose daily uniform consisted of corduroy slacks, a wrinkled oxford shirt, faded sweater, and sensible shoes. Instead she shrugged.

"Was that just her way of taking advantage of Martin Chastain's wealth?" Marcie asked.

"I don't think so. The clothes were nice but not extravagant, and most of the jewelry was just for show, costume pieces. I think she just liked variety in her wardrobe so she could dress up in different ways."

"Sounds like a little girl putting on her mother's clothes."

"I was thinking something similar. My guess is that she was a bit like an actress who liked to dress for different parts."

"I like to just be me," Marcie said, obviously savoring another piece of meat.

"Well, some people want to dramatize their lives."

"That just makes things more complicated."

"For some people more complicated means more exciting," Amanda said, feeling that she was in the midst of a losing struggle to get Marcie to understand a woman who was beyond her comprehension.

"Do you think she was sleeping with William Chastain?" Marcie asked.

Amanda barely kept the surprise from registering on her

face. Marcie might not be interested in subtleties of character, but she certainly could cut to the chase.

"I don't think so," Amanda replied.

"Why not? You thought his wife was kind of the mousy
type, and Larissa certainly sounds pretty glamorous. If they
went out to things together at night, wouldn't it be natural
for one thing to lead to another? Plus Nick told us earlier
that there was some talk about Larissa having an affair with
the golf pro at the country club, so maybe she did that kind
of thing regularly."

"If she was having an affair, I don't think it would be
with Will because I don't think he would get involved with
his father's wife. Will has spent his whole life trying to earn
his father's love. He wouldn't risk all hope of that by getting involved with his stepmother."

Marcie nodded. They finished eating in silence. When
Marcie suggested they get dessert, Amanda begged off and
said that it was getting close to the time for them to get ready
to meet Nick.

As they were walking up the stairs to their rooms, Marcie leaned closer to Amanda and whispered, "You know,
even if Will didn't sleep with his stepmother, he still might
have been jealous enough of her relationship with his father
to kill her."

Amanda nodded. "Then he'd certainly be motivated to
get into that coffin to find the clue—if there is one."

Chapter Fifteen

"Do you think that we should bring a weapon?" Marcie had asked as she followed Nick and Amanda out of the inn on the way to the cemetery.

"What did you have in mind?" Krow asked.

"I always carry a baseball bat in my car just in case," Marcie replied.

"In case of what?" Amanda asked.

Marcie shrugged. "You never know. You have to be prepared."

Amanda felt a disorienting sense of having underestimated her assistant once again. Her own vaguely formulated plan of using her car keys to strike at a potential attacker's eyes suddenly seemed woefully inadequate.

"Sure, bring it along," Krow had said offhandedly.

But now, as Ben opened the front door of his house and stared at the three figures arrayed in a row on his porch,

Krow felt slightly foolish. He could see himself through Ben's eyes, standing there with a Louisville slugger like he was going door to door looking for a nighttime pickup game in the middle of winter. Ben apparently didn't see any humor in the situation because his face remained blank until he saw Marcie. A smile lit up his face.

"C'mon in," he announced, stepping back and extending his arm with a flourish.

Nick glanced over at Amanda with a twinkle in his eye that said "looks like Marcie has an admirer." Amanda frowned in return, not being sure that this budding friendship was a good thing. As a newspaper reporter in the city, she'd often heard about offbeat friendships that ended in violence.

"Did you lock the gate behind you?" Ben asked Nick before he let him in the door. Ben had opened the gate earlier so they could drive inside and park by his house. Krow assured him that they had.

When the three of them had trooped into the front room, Amanda was surprised to find that the setting was quite domestic and cozy. A fire was blazing away in the large stone fireplace and a pleasant smell of freshly made bread filled the air. Not being much of a cook, Amanda felt herself transported back to her grandmother's kitchen in Boston and wanted nothing more than to curl up with a good book in front of the fire.

"I didn't know if you all would have eaten, so I took the liberty of making soup and baking some bread," Ben said, smiling and rubbing his hands together, managing to appear both dissolute and ingratiating at the same time.

"I should go right back outside. No sense in getting

warmed up, just to get cold again," Nick said, looking for an excuse to escape from Ben's unnerving attentiveness.

"Before you go, we should work out a schedule and some set of signals," said Amanda.

Krow frowned. "Signals?"

"How are we supposed to know if you're all right out there? The coffin vandal could hit you over the head, and we'd be sitting in here happily, not knowing that anything had happened."

"I have my cell phone. Do you have yours?"

Amanda nodded.

"I'll call every half hour and if I spot anything unusual."

"Fine. How long are you going to be out there? You can't stay out there all night by yourself. We have to pull shifts."

"How about I stay out from nine until midnight?"

Amanda shook her head. "It's too cold to be out there for three hours straight."

Nick sighed his impatience. "What do you suggest?"

"One hour shifts. That way we'll each get one hour on and two hours to sleep."

"That's not much consecutive sleep time."

"It adds up to the same amount."

Nick paused, then nodded. "I suppose you're right. I'll check in at nine-thirty."

"And I'll relieve you at ten," Amanda said, looking into the kitchen where Marcie and Ben were by the stove staring down into the pot of soup and discussing recipes. "I think Marcie will be able to keep busy until eleven. How will I know where you are?"

"I'll give you a couple of quick flashes on the light when I phone in so you can find me."

"Be careful," Amanda warned as Nick opened the door. "This could be a pretty desperate person we're dealing with."

"Don't worry, I'm not planning on being a hero. If I see anything, I'll call the police right away. Plus I always have this," he said, hefting the bat and giving Amanda a doubtful smile.

Just as the door closed, Marcie came out of the kitchen carrying a steaming bowl of soup and placed it on the small dining room table.

"Want some soup?" she asked. "It's beef barley. One of my favorites."

Amanda shook her head. She watched as Ben came out of the kitchen and took his place across from Marcie.

"Do you have a room where I can see the cemetery?" she asked him.

He nodded as he sliced the homemade bread with what looked to be a very sharp knife. Amanda wondered briefly whether she and Marcie were in more danger inside than Nick was outside.

"Go straight back next to the kitchen. It's a spare room that I don't use."

Amanda followed his directions. She opened the door and turned on the overhead light in a fairly large square room that was empty except for a plastic chair that was set up in front of the back window looking directly out on the cemetery. She turned out the light, and using the faint glow of moonlight coming through the window, made her way across the room and sat down. As she craned her neck to look up through the trees, Amanda saw that it was about a three-quarters moon. She hoped that Nick was careful to position himself so as not to be seen.

The dark silhouettes of the headstones backlit by the silvery moonlight had an austere, restful quality, and Amanda soon found her thoughts drifting away from Nick to her problems with Jeff. A decision had to be made in the next two days. Jeff would be leaving then, and no decision would be the same as making one. Even though he had smiled gamely when she asked for some time to consider, she could tell that his feelings had been hurt because she hadn't enthusiastically taken up his offer to go to D.C. with him.

Why didn't I? Amanda asked herself. It wasn't really because the offer hadn't come bundled with a proposal of marriage. That was more of an excuse to give Marcie. They'd never discussed their future that way, and if Jeff had proposed, she was sure that her uncertainly as to what to do would only have increased. But why? She liked Jeff. He had that quality of understated ambition that she preferred in a man. He wanted to succeed in his chosen profession but not at the expense of sacrificing every other aspect of his life. He would always make time for having fun and to develop his interests outside of the practice of law. He also recognized that her career was important as well, and she was sure that he'd be willing to find a compromise if their career goals should ever conflict.

Amanda knew that a psychologist would say that her reluctance to commit was due to having an alcoholic father and an emotionally distant mother—parents who had created a family setting for Amanda and her brothers that made them feel constantly insecure. Demonstrating as only childhood lessons can that relationships are undependable and a poor source of support. As Amanda sat looking out on the headstones forming geometric patterns in the moonlight, she rejected that view of her mental life as too simplistic. Her reluctance to commit couldn't be reduced to an unstable home life because to believe that was to ignore her uniqueness, leaving her as nothing more than an illustrative case study.

No, whatever the reason for her hesitation might be for not leaping at the chance to live with Jeff, it was due to something specific to their relationship, and couldn't be completely explained away as another instance of a pathological failure to commit. Amanda settled down as deeply as she could in the hard plastic chair and decided that it was time to carefully reexamine how she felt about Jeff.

Ben cut another piece of bread and gently, even lovingly, placed it next to Marcie's plate. Marcie nodded her thanks, surprised that she didn't feel the least bit uncomfortable dining alone with a man who saw sea monsters and vampires. She found it hard to be afraid of someone whose actions were so considerate, even deferential. *Maybe this is what they mean about judging people by their deeds rather than their words,* she thought.

She leaned over her bowl of soup, savoring the aroma, then began to quickly spoon it into her mouth. When she finally looked up, Ben was watching her with a smile as he chewed on a piece of bread.

"You sure do like your food," he said.

Marcie blushed. "Is there anything wrong with that?"

Ben shook his head rapidly. "Nope. You can't trust people

who don't eat like they enjoy it." He paused, as if unsure whether to continue.

"What is it?" Marcie asked.

"You can't trust people who sneak around either."

"Who does that?"

The old man sucked in his lips as if tasting the words before saying them.

"That boy you've been hanging around with."

"What boy?"

"That cop."

"Kirk Ames?"

"That's the one."

It was Marcie's turn to pause, not sure that she wanted to hear anything negative about Kirk. Even though she had soured a bit on their relationship, some part of her still hoped that things could be worked out between them. Finally, however, her need to know overpowered her fear of being completely disillusioned with the handsomest man who had ever shown an interest in her.

"Where was he sneaking around?"

"It's *who* he was sneaking around that's important. I saw him hanging around that Larissa Chastain."

"What do you mean?" A quick flare of jealousy made Marcie's voice sharp.

"Now don't get mad at me, missy. It's not my fault that this guy is a no good, lying hound."

"Where did you see all this?" she asked more calmly.

"Up at the lake, at the Chastain cottage. He used to go out there in his own car and park under the trees last summer. It would have been pretty hard to spot it from the road, but I could see it pretty plain from out on the lake."

"And you saw Mrs. Chastain there too?"

"Yep. She was there all right. Sometimes they were there together the whole afternoon." He grinned showing the frequent spaces where his teeth were missing. "Just goes to show that if you've got a wife like that it doesn't pay to spend your whole time working."

Marcie bent over her soup again and ate a couple more spoonfuls, although it was one of the few times when she hardly tasted anything. Ben watched her with a worried expression, as if regretting that he'd told her about Kirk.

"Haven't see his car up there since late summer," he said finally. "Guess they broke it off."

"Or went somewhere else," Marcie said, staring down glumly at her soup.

"Yeah. There's always that."

When she felt calm enough to look up again, Ben was gazing across the room with a fixed expression on his face. He shivered and rubbed his arms as if cold, although the room was overheated by the fire.

"Course I wouldn't have been surprised by anything that woman did—if she was a woman, that is."

"What are you talking about?"

"Always walking through the cemetery at night like she'd rather be with the dead than with the living."

"When was this?" Marcie asked.

Ben frowned. "From around the end of the summer to a few weeks before she died. I even caught her once and asked what she was doing wandering around in my cemetery. She got all high and mighty and told me to mind my own business or she'd have me fired. If I was your friend out there tonight, I'd be real careful. Maybe there wasn't anyone trying to get into that coffin. Maybe that was her trying to get out."

Amanda's phone bleated, breaking her train of thought, which had been going around and around pointlessly on the subject of Jeff. She glanced at her watch as she answered and was surprised to see that a half hour had passed.

"Having a good time chatting with Ben?" Nick asked.

"I'm sitting all by myself in the back room looking out at the cemetery. Marcie and Ben are probably busy swapping recipes."

"I can see the back of the building. Let me show you where I am."

Amanda saw a quick flash of light off to her right.

"Got you. How are things out there?"

"A little cold. You were right, staying out here longer than an hour would be too much. Maybe you and Marcie should limit yourselves to half an hour each."

"Then you won't get much sleep," Amanda objected.

"I've got to hang up now," Nick whispered with sudden urgency. "I think I see someone coming."

"Should I call the police?"

"Let me make sure first that there's really someone there. I'll get back to you."

"Be careful," Amanda said, but the connection had already been cut off.

Nick stared into the darkness waiting for another glimpse of the shape he had seen moving against the moonlight. He was about to give up and call Amanda back to say that it had just been a trick of the imagination, when he saw a figure rise up from behind one of the headstones and glide in the direction of the Chastain mausoleum. Slipping out from the shadow of the evergreen where he had been hiding, Krow ran forward, staying slightly bent over and hoping that he'd blend in with the profile of the headstones should the person he was following look back.

He knelt down on the hard earth behind a stone that was about twenty feet from the front door of the mausoleum, which was shrouded in shadows. No one seemed to be moving in the darkness. Krow debated whether to call the police, but decided that he wanted to be certain that someone actually was trying to break into the mausoleum before making the call. He'd have enough explaining to do to the chief after a legitimate call without raising a false alarm. Not being able to see the doors of the building was frustrating, so he took a chance and slowly edged forward, on the alert for any movement around him. He was out in the moonlight now, so he'd be easy to spot. He clutched the baseball bat tightly in his right hand, almost wishing he didn't have it. He wasn't sure that he could really hit someone, and it might just get in the way and slow him down if he had to defend himself.

About six feet from the front of the mausoleum, he stepped on a dead branch that cracked like a pistol shot on the cold night air. Before he could react, someone came hurtling forward out of the darkness. Krow felt something hit his shoulder and ricochet off his temple. Instinctively he dropped the bat and reached out to grab what had hit him. He felt something thin and metallic in his hand and pulled hard on it. There was a brief tug of war, then Krow found himself toppling backward with the object in his hands.

Tossing the thing to one side, he struggled to his feet in

time to see a figure silhouetted in the moonlight going over
the rise behind the mausoleum. Krow began to give chase.
Dodging around the headstones, he struggled to pull his
flashlight out of his coat pocket but it caught on the lining,
and he was unwilling to stop running long enough to free it.
Krow cleared the rise and finally could see the fence surrounding the cemetery and the lights on the street where the
intruder had probably parked his car. He saw the back gates
to the cemetery and thought he spotted a dark figure slither
between the post and the gate. Krow picked up speed, hoping to at least spot the vehicle before it pulled away. His
breath was raspy and the cold hurt his lungs, but the ground
in front of him appeared to be mercifully free of headstones, so he forced himself to break into a sprint.

He had taken three steps when he hit something hard
with his left foot. Before he was even aware of what had
happened, he was sprawled out flat on the ground with the
wind knocked out of him. It took him several seconds before he could breathe again and even longer to climb to his
feet. By then he was certain the intruder was long gone. He
pulled out the flashlight and slowly examined the ground. A
few feet behind him he saw it: a memorial marker flat to the
ground with an attached metal vase that stuck up about a
foot. It held a bouquet of plastic flowers.

"Tripped up by bad taste," he muttered to himself.

As he started to make his way back to Ben's, he saw a
light cautiously coming across the cemetery toward him.
He called out, and a moment later Amanda was standing in
front of him.

"Are you okay?" she asked.

"I was doing fine until I tripped."

"Were you chasing someone?"

"Yeah. I spotted a guy trying to get into the mausoleum. We struggled, but he got away."

"Are you okay?"

"I'm fine."

"Any idea who it was?"

"Not a clue. But whoever it was moved pretty fast."

The sound of sirens began to echo in the distance.

"I called the police when you hung up. I wasn't sure that you were going to do it," Amanda said with a note of reprimand.

"A good thing you did. I meant to, but by the time I was sure there was someone poking around the mausoleum, I didn't have the chance."

Krow reached up and felt something wet on his forehead.

"Feels like I got hit on the head."

Amanda came closer and directed her flashlight to his forehead. She took a tissue out of her pocket and wiped away the blood.

"It doesn't look bad. You have a small cut."

Nick took the tissue from her and dabbed gingerly at his wound.

"I think whatever I got hit with is back by the mausoleum. That might give us at least one clue as to who I was chasing. We'd better head back and explain things to the police."

"I don't think the chief is going to be happy with us for doing this."

Krow nodded. "I have a feeling that explaining things to him will end up hurting worse than this cut on my head."

The two of them arrived back at the mausoleum just in

time to meet Chief Toth and Kirk Ames coming toward them from the direction of Ben's house. The police officers directed strong beams of light in both their faces for a long time as they approached. Krow wasn't sure whether it was some kind of punishment or whether they really were struggling to recognize them.

"Well, Ms. Vickers and Professor Krow," Chief Toth finally said with patently false joviality. "What are the two of you doing out here?"

Although his tone was bantering, it was clear that he was less than happy. When Krow finished explaining what had taken place, Toth told Kirk to search the area around the mausoleum for whatever had been used to hit Krow. Then he suggested that they all go back to Ben's house for a chat, which Amanda guessed was his folksy term for an interrogation. He offered to call an ambulance if Nick thought he needed medical attention, but Krow said that wouldn't be necessary.

When they walked into the living room of Ben's house, Marcie jumped up and rushed toward them.

"Are you all right?" she asked Nick, staring at the streak of blood on his forehead.

"It's just a bump."

Marcie disappeared into the kitchen and came back in a moment with a damp cloth. She wiped his head, then handed him a small plastic bag filled with ice.

"This should help bring down the swelling."

Nick thanked her, then took a seat by the chief and Amanda near the fire.

"So you decided to play detective," the chief said, giving Krow a hard look.

Nick shrugged. "It just occurred to me this afternoon that if Martin Chastain was going to have Larissa's coffin examined tomorrow, it might motivate our intruder to try to break into the mausoleum tonight. I knew you were having patrols check on the place, but I figured that it would be pretty easy for someone to slip in there between rounds."

"If you'd called me with your idea, I might have been pretty easily convinced to station a man there all night."

"I wasn't sure that anything was going to happen."

"But you were hoping it would, so you could play the hero."

Krow frowned.

"That's not quite fair, chief," Amanda said. "Nick told me to call the police as soon as he saw anything. And don't forget, if it wasn't for Nick, someone might have ransacked Larissa's coffin tonight and you'd have to explain that to Martin Chastain in the morning."

The chief pursed his lips, which Amanda took as a small concession.

"Did you get a look at your attacker?" he asked.

Krow shook his head.

"Too bad. I talked to that boy at the hospital today, and he can't give me a description either."

The door to the house opened, and Kirk entered. In one gloved hand he held a baseball bat and in the other a pair of long-handled nippers.

"The baseball bat is mine," Krow said with an embarrassed smile.

"Then those are what must have been used in the attack on you," Chief Toth said, indicating the nippers. "He was planning to use them to cut off the padlock. Those points are pretty sharp. It's a good thing that guy didn't get a clear shot at you."

"Too bad you didn't put that baseball bat to some good use," Kirk said. "Then we might have this guy by now."

Krow looked at the officer, but said nothing.

"Was the chain on the mausoleum cut?" Toth asked.

Kirk shook his head.

The chief sighed. "Well, you scared him off before he could do any damage. At least that's something. But I guess it's a good thing that you'll all be leaving tomorrow."

"I'm afraid we won't, chief," Krow said. "I've promised Will Chastain that I'd be there with his father when the mortician checks out the coffin."

"What about the two of you?" Chief Toth said, looking at the two women.

Amanda glanced at Nick, who was giving her an imploring smile.

"I'd like to stay around tomorrow and see what's discovered in the coffin," Amanda said.

"I'm with her," Marcie said cheerfully.

The chief slowly got to his feet.

"Well, I can't prevent you from being present tomorrow, especially if the family wants you. But I hope that if you discover anything or come up with any more bright ideas in the future that you'll run them by me first."

"Sure will," Krow said with a smile.

The chief stared at him a moment longer as if wondering whether to believe him, then he turned toward the door.

"I think we should all call it a night now, and leave Ben in peace."

Ben was standing back in the doorway of the kitchen as

if hoping to remain unnoticed and had said nothing during the entire encounter.

"Think you can get any fingerprints off of those nippers?" Nick asked as he put on his coat.

"Don't you think that the perp would have worn gloves on a cold night like this?" Kirk snapped.

"We'll check," the chief said more moderately. "But I don't hold out much hope."

Marcie waved to Ben and thanked him. He gave her a sad smile, obviously sad to see her go.

"No more visitors tonight," Kirk said, turning back to Ben after everyone else had left the house. "Remember, I'm watching you."

Ben stared at him blankly as if he hadn't spoken.

Kirk fell into step beside Marcie, who was walking behind the others.

"You're hanging out with a couple of troublemakers," he warned her in a low voice. "Don't let them get you to do anything you shouldn't."

Marcie gave him a sharp glance. "They're my friends and coworkers, and nobody gets me to do anything I don't want to do," she replied, giving each word a special emphasis.

"What's the matter with you, Marcie?" Kirk asked in frustration. "I thought we were getting along pretty well, and now all of a sudden you act like you can't stand the sight of me."

"Look, I don't think there's any point in discussing it. You just turned out to be a different person than I thought you were. That's my mistake, not yours. Let's just leave it at that."

Before Kirk could say more, Marcie ran the last few

yards and slid into the back seat of the car. Nick was holding the door and closed it behind her. He glanced at Kirk,
who seemed ready to follow Marcie into the car to continue
the discussion. Finally Kirk gave a helpless shrug and
headed over to the police cruiser.

"Quite a night," Krow said after he got in the car. Not
getting any response from either of the women, he gave his
own shrug and turned the key in the ignition.

Chapter Sixteen

Some people lose their appetites when they're unhappy, Marcie thought, *I'm not even that lucky. When I'm happy, I eat; when I'm depressed, I eat more.* She looked down at her plate, a platter really, which was covered with food: a three-egg omelet, thick-cut toast, bacon, and home fries. It was called the lumberjack special, but Marcie doubted that even lumberjacks ate like that on a regular basis. If they did, they'd be too full to go out and deforest the wilderness.

She gave a deep sigh, then began to eat. She had felt empowered last night after rejecting Kirk, as if she had struck a blow for plain women everywhere by showing that she didn't need an obnoxious, if handsome, man in her life. But in the morning as she lay in bed staring up at the ceiling and trying to talk herself into her morning run, she had regrets at what in the calm light of dawn seemed to have been a hasty act. Did she really have to burn her bridges quite so dramatically? Couldn't she have been a tad more concilia-tory toward Kirk while at the same time making her dis-pleasure clear? So what if he'd had a relationship with Larissa Chastain? By all accounts she was a beautiful and charming woman, and Kirk was certainly a handsome guy. Okay, Larissa was married, but maybe she had seduced him. Men were notoriously weak that way.

Of course, that didn't change the fact that Kirk was something of a bully, especially in his handling of Ben. But he was a cop after all, and one of the natural dangers of the job, she imagined, was a tendency to be a bit abrupt with people. And Ben was the type of character who might natu-rally draw police attention. Even though she found herself attracted to Ben as a kind of grandfatherly figure, there was no denying that he had a creepy side to him.

"Comfort food?" Amanda said, sliding into the chair across from Marcie and eyeing her half-empty plate.

"I suppose," Marcie said sullenly.

"What's the problem?" Amanda asked quickly. Her asso-ciate was so rarely out of sorts that when it happened there was usually good reason for concern.

Not waiting to be asked twice, Marcie quickly revealed the new information she had learned about Kirk, and went on to express her doubts about whether she should have made her break with Kirk quite so final.

Amanda shook her head firmly. "Don't give it a second thought. The other day when you were so certain that dumping Kirk was a good idea because of the way he treated Ben I wasn't so sure. But this puts everything in a new light. He's a man who would have a secret affair with another man's wife. You don't want to get involved with someone like that. You'd never be able to trust him."

"I suppose."

"And, of course, we have to consider the possibility that he might be the killer of Larissa Chastain."

Marcie's eyes popped open wide. "Do you really think so?"

"Actually, no," Amanda admitted after a moment's thought.

"Why not?" asked Marcie, sounding offended that her almost boyfriend couldn't be a cold-blooded killer. "I can imagine lots of good reasons for him to kill her."

Amanda waited for the waitress to pour coffee and take her order of a cup of oatmeal and a dry English muffin. She took a long sip of coffee and gave Marcie a level look.

"What reasons?"

"Well, what if she threatened to tell her husband about their affair?" Marcie asked. "If that happened then the chief of police would find out, and he'd probably fire Kirk."

"Why would she do that?"

"Maybe she was in love with Kirk and wanted him to marry her. If he refused, she might see telling her husband as a way to force his hand."

Amanda shook her head. "I don't know much about Larissa, but she doesn't sound to me like the kind of woman who would give up the Chastain money and lifetstyle for an unemployed police officer, no matter how young and hand-some he is."

Marcie frowned for a moment. "Okay, maybe you're right about that. But what if Larissa got pregnant and knew the baby was Kirk's. Maybe then she'd be willing to give up everything in order to have her baby live with its father."

Amanda stared into Marcie's doelike eyes and smiled gently.

"Life isn't usually like a romance novel. If Larissa were pregnant by Kirk, which she wasn't or the chief would have told us, she'd be more likely to claim that the baby was Martin's in order to get in on the inheritance."

Marcie savagely cut off another chunk of omelet and shoved it in her mouth.

"Maybe I haven't got it right yet. But I still think it's possible that Kirk did it."

"He'd be more likely to murder Martin Chastain than Larissa. I can see Kirk wanting to marry a wealthy widow."

Marcie's eyes lit up. "What if Larissa wanted to break it off with Kirk, and she said something humiliating to him. Then he got angry and killed her on the spur of the moment? What if it was a crime of passion?"

"That theory would work better if her body had been found out at the cottage on Lake Opal or in some motel room, but it doesn't really fit in with Larissa being killed while she was on a shopping trip in Portland."

"What if they weren't just meeting at the cottage, but got together somewhere in Portland?" Marcie went on gamely. "What if Kirk killed her there in a moment of rage, and then dumped her body in the street to make it look like a robbery gone wrong?"

Amanda's oatmeal arrived. She carefully added raisins, brown sugar, a little milk, and stirred it together into a grainy mass. She put a small spoonful in her mouth and closed her eyes.

"They make good oatmeal here, nice and creamy."

"I don't know how you can eat that stuff. Out West we only give it to horses."

"I like it, and it helps lower cholesterol. High cholesterol runs in my family."

"Do you have high cholesterol?" Marcie asked.

Amanda shook her head. "But then I eat lots of oatmeal."

Marcie was about to object to that reasoning when she saw the teasing smile on Amanda's face. Reluctantly she grinned back at her friend.

"So you think that I should lighten up about Kirk being a killer?"

'I'm not saying that you're definitely wrong, but I don't think we should get out the shackles for him just yet."

"Should I tell Chief Toth about his affair with Larissa?"

"When you go off a man, you really go off him, don't you?" Amanda said. "A few minutes ago you were thinking about getting back with him. Now you want to destroy his career."

"That was before you put it in my head that he could be a murderer. But, really, don't you think that the chief should know? I mean you and Nick were practically working for the guy. Don't you think you have a responsibility to tell him that one of his officers was involved with a murder victim?"

"All you have is a story from Ben, who has good reason to dislike Kirk."

A rebellious expression passed over Marcie's face, and Amanda held up her hand.

"But I agree with you. Since we are working with the chief, we have to report what Ben said. It will be up to the chief to evaluate the evidence and decide whether to pursue it or not. I'll let him know when I see him at the opening of Larissa's coffin, if I go."

"If you go? I thought that was a definite."

Amanda chewed a piece of her English muffin and stared across the room. Several of the other tables were occupied. An older couple was sitting in the far corner leafing through brochures that they'd probably gotten from the lobby, trying to work out a sightseeing plan for the day. Near by two younger women wearing jeans and sweaters were talking about some men they had met in a bar the night before. She wondered briefly what it would be like to feel as free and relaxed as other people seemed.

Amanda sighed.

"We really should get back to the office."

"But we'll be leaving right in the middle of an exciting story."

"One we'll never get to write about unless it connects with the séance. But even if we could work in a paranormal aspect, this story doesn't feel right for us. The whole thing is too recent. You know we generally confine ourselves to folklore or strange happenings from the past. Writing about this would be too close to a true crime sort of thing, which isn't our cup of tea."

"I kind of said all of this yesterday when you suggested that we look into the Chastain story," Marcie pointed out.

"Yes, I guess you did."

Marcie eyed her friend thoughtfully. Amanda was being uncharacteristically indecisive. She suspected it was because this business with Jeff had thrown her for a loop, even though Amanda would never have admitted it.

"We really have no excuse to stay. I talked to Greg

yesterday," Amanda continued, referring to the managing editor, "and he said that we should stay as long as we think is necessary. But I don't want to abuse his generosity. I'm sure he's been working overtime to take up some of the slack while we're away. So I suppose we should go back home."

Amanda paused. She felt guilty about staying in West Windham when there seemed to be no legitimate story, but returning to Wells would bring her closer to having to make a decision about Jeff. Being away somehow seemed to justify putting her daily concerns on hold, allowing her to pretend that a solution to her dilemma would magically appear at the last minute. *I'm just playing psychological tricks on myself,* she thought scornfully. But then the Chastain story was genuinely fascinating, and even if it wouldn't work in the magazine, she hated to leave before following up on all the leads.

"Of course, you haven't been out to see Lake Opal for yourself," Marcie said, as if she could read her mind. "Maybe we should go there together."

"You're writing the story. I'm not sure it's important that I see it," Amanda said, not sure she wanted to seize the lifeline Marcie was throwing her.

"Two pairs of eyes are always better than one. Not that I expect we'll spot the monster, but I think the atmosphere of the lake will play a big part in what I write. In fact, since we don't have much of a description of the monster, the entire story will be pretty much history mixed with a little atmosphere. I'd really like to get your perspective."

Amanda studied her friend's face to see if Marcie had guessed why she didn't want to return to Wells. She wondered whether her friend was intentionally offering her an excuse to stay away. But the expression on Marcie's face showed nothing but professional interest.

"Okay, why don't we go there this morning since I'm supposed to accompany Nick to the mortuary this afternoon to look at Larissa's body. I was going to beg off and say we had to get back, but maybe I owe it to Nick to accompany him."

"Are you really going to *look* at her?" Marcie asked, wrinkling her nose as if the smell of formaldehyde and decay was seeping across the dining room.

"I don't know. I doubt that Martin will want to make this into a public spectacle. Nick wants me along to study people's reactions, not to examine the corpse. But since Will Chastain has appointed him as his stand-in to make sure that somebody gives an objective report of what they find, I suppose Nick wants me to serve as a second set of eyes. That may include being there when the coffin is opened."

"Better you than me."

Amanda smiled. "I'll tell Nick you want to do it next time."

"Don't you dare," Marcie said, sticking out her tongue. "I wonder what sort of clue the ghost was talking about?"

"Probably a ghostly kind that will remain invisible to everyone," Amanda said.

"The guy who hit Nick last night doesn't think so."

"That's true," Amanda admitted, wondering once again why a killer would be so quick to believe in ghosts.

"So maybe you really will find something in the coffin?"

Amanda savored her last spoonful of oatmeal.

"If we do, let's hope that it's something clear like a note giving the name of the killer."

Chapter Seventeen

K row sat in the window of the bakery and gently rubbed his forehead. He'd placed a bandage over the cut, but the bump about the size of a half dollar surrounding it couldn't be concealed. He realized that he was vain enough to wonder if his injury made him look rugged or just clumsy, and smiled to himself at this piece of self-awareness.

The bakery had several tables in the front where patrons could eat a morning pastry and drink their coffee, and that's where Krow was, reading the local paper and enjoying a blueberry muffin. He knew a nutritionist would have told him that a healthy breakfast at the restaurant in the inn was better preparation for viewing a corpse, but he figured that he could take care of that with a nutritious early lunch. Plus this was a good way to avoid dissecting last night's events with Amanda and Marcie.

Touching the bump once again, he had to admit to himself

that the main reason he didn't want to discuss things with the women was because he was ashamed of his poor performance in the cemetery last night. He'd have had a good chance to learn the identity of the person breaking into the Chastain mausoleum if he hadn't stupidly tried to apprehend him. If he had been more patient and waited until the intruder had left the tomb and headed back to his car, he could easily have followed him and gotten his license plate number to give to the police.

All he had accomplished was to scare the thief away. On the bright side, at least nothing had been removed from the coffin. That was the one achievement that kept him from being truly disgusted with himself, but on the other hand, he had been outfought and outrun by his adversary. As a competitor on the athletic field since childhood, he felt that the bump on his head was proof that the other guy had gotten the better of him. A silly point of view, perhaps, but it was all part of the masculine package that Krow guessed had some benefits.

A familiar face turned from the bakery counter and their eyes locked for an instant, long enough that Krow couldn't pretend not to have recognized him without being rude. The other man clearly felt the same.

"Hello," Eric Devlin said, coming over to Krow's table. "I see you've found one of the best local places. Mind if I join you?"

"Not at all." Krow moved the morning paper to one side.

"Any good news?" Devlin asked, glancing at the headlines as he placed his coffee and a cheese danish down on the table.

"War, disease, and government corruption. All the usual

hot topics," Nick replied, reluctantly putting aside the story he'd been reading and telling himself that he should be grilling Devlin as a possible suspect.

The other man sipped his coffee and looked with curiosity at Krow's face. He tapped his own forehead.

"Barroom brawl?"

"Graveyard brawl, actually," Krow said and described the events of last evening.

"Any idea who it was?" Devlin asked.

Krow shook his head. "No idea."

Devlin stirred some half-and-half into his coffee, carefully watching it lighten. Then he looked up at Krow.

"You were there the night of the séance. Why would anyone believe what that crazy old woman said?"

"I gather you were less than impressed with Mrs. Narapov."

"To me it was a bunch of hooey. But you're the expert. What did you think?"

"It was pretty standard stuff—until the end."

"What do you mean?"

"Well, usually these mediums give pretty vague predictions, so they can't be proven wrong. But she told us exactly where to go for a clue. Mrs. Narapov is going to look pretty bad this afternoon if there's nothing out of the ordinary in the coffin."

"So you think that we'll find something?"

Krow shrugged. "I'm not saying that. I'm just saying that it won't look good for her if we don't. By the way, you said 'we.' Are you going to be there this afternoon?"

Devlin gave an embarrassed smile. "Yeah, Martin asked me to go with him since Will refused to attend."

"Chastain expects a lot from his financial adviser."

"I'm actually a little more than that."

"A substitute son," Nick suggested.

The man frowned. "In a way, I guess you could say so. I know that doesn't sound very good since Martin's already got a perfectly good son who's devoted to him. But I guess Martin and I have always had more in common with each other than he has with Will. We both have an interest in business, and we enjoy strategizing and coming up with new marketing ideas."

"I thought you were his personal financial adviser. I didn't realize that you had anything to do with his business."

"I don't, at least not officially."

"How did the two of you meet?"

"We met at a party here in town five years ago when I was working for one of the banks. We took to each other right away, and a few months later, when I told Martin that I wanted to go out on my own as a financial consultant, he said that he'd be my first client and direct other business my way. He was as good as his word. Over the last few years, I've also served as a sort of outside consultant for some aspects of his business. I don't go to board meetings or anything like that, but we get together for a drink once a week or so and talk about things."

Krow nodded. "Since the two of you are so close, what do you make of his sudden interest in contacting Larissa?"

Devlin carefully wiped his fingers with the napkin before answering.

"It worries me as much as it worries Will. I was stunned when Martin announced the idea. It came from out of nowhere. He'd never discussed it with me beforehand. He sprang it on all of us. Will and I even got together and talked about it after we'd heard. We were both wondering whether it was a sign of developing dementia or whether Martin had suffered some kind of small stroke. But his mind is as sharp as ever. There are no signs of forgetfulness or misunderstanding complicated concepts. He'd just developed this fixation with contacting Larissa's ghost."

"What was your opinion of Larissa?"

Devlin grinned. "She was the stereotype of a rich man's second wife. She was beautiful, flirtatious, dramatic, and she seemed to dote on Martin."

"I've heard that she might have played around on him."

"Oh, you mean that golf club story. Martin never believed that and neither did I. Men tended to exaggerate her flirtatious behavior into more than it was. They each thought that the other guy was getting what they wanted, when in reality none of them were except for Martin. She was very loyal to him."

"Had she been married before?" asked Krow.

"Yes, when she was in her early twenties. I think it was brief. All she ever said about it was that it was a mistake and they both knew it right away. I guess that was when she was living out in California. That's where she grew up."

"Do you agree with the police that her murder was a robbery gone bad?"

Devlin's eyes widened in surprise. "Of course. What else could it have been?"

"I was just wondering if someone who knew her might have had a reason to want her dead."

"The thought never occurred to me. I can't come up with a reason why anyone would want to kill Larissa."

Krow nodded. "It's just that if this was a random crime on the streets of Portland by a career criminal, how did the killer know that the medium said there was a clue hidden in Larissa's coffin? That seems to suggest that the killer is someone who stays in close contact with the Chastain family."

"Of course, you must be right." Devlin said slowly as he finished his coffee and got to his feet. "But that doesn't help you very much in figuring who it might be. There are lots of people at the company and even around town who have probably heard stories about a medium being called. Martin hasn't been very discreet about the whole thing, as much as Will and I have begged him to keep it quiet."

"But only those of us at the séance knew what the message was on the same night that it was delivered. Did you talk to anyone that night about what happened?"

Devlin shook his head. "One of the things you learn in my profession is the importance of discretion."

"Well, maybe whatever is in the coffin will identify the killer for us."

"Let's hope so," Devlin said, giving Krow a parting nod.

"How far is it to Lake Opal?" Amanda asked.

"Around eight miles," Marcie replied, navigating the twisting road with all the confidence of a grand prix driver.

"People from West Windham have summer homes only eight miles from town? That isn't much of a getaway."

"Kirk said that most of the cottages have been in the same families for years. I guess back in the horse and buggy days eight miles was pretty far, and folks just wanted a place to go that was on a lake."

Amanda nodded and sat back, enjoying the view. It was a clear, sunny day with large puffy clouds sailing grandly across the sky. The sun warmed the inside of the car, but there was enough wind to make it feel brisk outside. A day away from work, she told herself. A sense of illicit freedom washed over her, and she felt like a little girl cutting school. She knew she should be back at the office putting the final touches on the next edition of the magazine and dealing in a mature, adult way with Jeff. But not doing either of those things made the morning seem even brighter and gave her a luxuriant appreciation of being alive on such a glorious day.

At a sign that announced LAKE OPAL Marcie turned off onto a newly paved road that led through a long stretch of forest until suddenly the trees thinned. Amanda found herself looking out on one of the most picturesque lakes that she had ever seen—a living picture postcard. Marcie drove another mile and then pulled off to the side into a public parking area. The road was a bit above the lake, so they were looking down on what appeared to be a giant basin created by the hills and filled with blue-green water.

"Can we walk down to the lake, or is it all private property?" Amanda asked.

"There's a public access trail all around the lake. We can walk down any of the marked paths from the public parking areas."

"Let's go," Amanda said, jumping out of the car.

Marcie smiled to herself at the girlish excitement in the voice of her usually calm and sophisticated boss. She hopped out of the car and followed Amanda down to the lake. Soon they were standing on a low promontory, gazing in both directions along the length of Lake Opal.

"How large is it?" Amanda asked. The wind was blowing her blond hair back behind her ears and her eyes were watering from looking into the wind, but there was a relaxed, happy smile on her face.

"Ben said it was three miles long and about a mile across."

"It's beautiful." Amanda stared across at the houses that were sprinkled along the shoreline on the other side. "Those places are huge. Is that what they call cottages?"

Marcie nodded. "I guess back in the nineteenth century your summer mansion was always called a cottage. That one over there belongs to Martin Chastain," she said, pointing to a large chaletlike building almost directly across from them. A driveway came down from where the road circled around the lake to a garage and small parking area. A dock extended out into the lake where a small motorboat was moored.

"So that's where Kirk and Larissa got together?" Amanda asked.

"According to Ben. You can't tell much from here, but I imagine that in the summer when the trees are out, you could hide a car from the road pretty easily near the garage"

"But not from the lake side."

"Just like Ben said."

Marcie pointed to a steep finger of land that came down into the lake on their right.

"Do you see how sharply the sides of that slope reach right to the water?"

"Yes."

"Well, according to Kirk that hillside gets hit particularly hard by the wind in the winter. I think it faces northwest. No one really understands it, I guess, but every winter a few trees fall and sort of slide down the slope and into the lake when the spring rains come. This is a spring-fed lake, and I guess it has a pretty strong current. So once the trees get out into the lake they start floating around."

"Must be a real headache for people who go boating. Why don't they just clear all the trees off the slope?"

"It would make the view from the other side pretty ugly. Instead they've tried to warn people. You can see the lines of red buoys out there to mark the patterns where the trees usually travel."

"Does it work?"

Marcie shook her head. "Not very well. The floating trees are too unpredictable. That's why a lot of people don't even bother boating on the lake, and if they do, they take it kind of slow."

"Not a very good solution to the problem," Amanda said.

"It isn't. But you know how things are in New England, everybody just says, 'we've always done it this way,' and they put up with it."

"Maybe that's why all the property hasn't been bought up by wealthy folks from down in Boston or New York."

"Most likely. It also explains something else. Can you guess?"

Amanda paused, then smiled in understanding. "That's how the stories about the monster got started."

Marcie nodded. "I guess a floating log can look a lot like a sea serpent under the right conditions. And probably plenty of boats have been sunk or damaged that way over the last hundred years or more. That's the more scientific theory about how the legend grew up."

"You'll have to include that view in your article," Amanda said. "We can let people choose for themselves which version of the events they want to believe."

"That's what I figured too. I think people kind of like it when there's a scientific explanation and a paranormal one. It sort of makes their minds jump around."

"Why don't we take a little walk in that direction," Amanda said, pointing to the right. "We've got plenty of time."

The two women went along at a good pace pointing out various cottages on the other side of the lake and commenting on them. They had gone about half a mile when a man suddenly came around a bend heading toward them. He was facing toward the lake, looking in the direction of the Chastain house, and didn't notice them until Amanda spoke.

"Hello, Will."

The man gave a start, then smiled when he recognized her.

"Amanda . . . Vickers, am I right?"

Amanda nodded and introduced Will Chastain to Marcie.

"I would have expected you to be hard at work," Amanda said with a smile. But the man looked so immediately guilty that she regretted her little joke.

"I hardly ever take a day off," he replied. "You have to be careful about that sort of thing when your father is the boss. People think you're taking advantage. But I couldn't very well go in today because everyone would wonder why I wasn't with my father at the mortician's. I hear that you're going to be there with Nick."

"I can't say that I'm looking forward to it."

"Who would? It's a ghastly thing."

He was about to say more, but then seemed to realize that

any further comments would sound critical of his father. So instead he sighed and looked across the lake.

"I didn't want to spend the day at home with Bethany and the children. I was too on edge to be good company, so I decided to come out here."

"To the family cottage?" Marcie asked, looking back at the Chastain house that was still clearly visible.

"That's my father's cottage. Mine is over there," he said, pointing just behind him to a boxy-looking modern structure which seemed to extend out from the side of the slope on stilts.

A bit of rebellion against his father's domination, Amanda thought. It would be hard to imagine anything more unlike his father's traditional-style home.

"It's very nice. Did you design it yourself?"

Will nodded, then blushed. "I always thought I'd enjoy being an architect. Of course, I had a professional help me with the design, but much of the concept is my own."

"And it's almost right across the lake from your father's house," Marcie said.

He nodded. "Dad gave me the property after I got married. He'd purchased it years ago when my mother was alive. That's when he bought his house. But his was already there. He didn't design it."

Amanda nodded to show that she got his point that there were things he could do that his father couldn't. It was sad to see a man in his thirties who was still in vigorous competition with his father, but maybe that never stopped, especially if your father was someone as successful as Martin.

"Do you get to spend much time here at the lake?" she asked.

"No. My dad is a bit of a workaholic, and I like to be there with him. So I don't really get to take much time off. The rest of the family spends most of the summer out here, and I usually join them at night after work. That's one advantage in having a summer home that's not very far away." Will was about to say more, then stopped, perhaps realizing that he'd already talked more about himself than usual. "Are you just out here sightseeing?"

"Marcie is working on a story about the Monster of Lake Opal, so we're doing the last of the research," Amanda answered.

The man smiled. "Hard to do research on something that doesn't exist."

"But you've heard the stories," Marcie said.

"Oh, sure. Anyone who's spent much time around the lake knows about the monster. If your family has a boat, the monster is used like a bogeyman when you're a child to keep you from speeding on the lake. Instead of saying 'watch out for floating trees' they'll say 'Go slow! Don't let the monster get you.'"

"But I take it that you've never seen anything weird?" Marcie asked.

William shook his head. "I've seen some funny looking trees go floating by sometimes, but never anything that would qualify as a prehistoric serpent."

"Have you known anyone who did see it?" Marcie persisted.

Will paused, as if unsure whether he wanted to say more about such a frivolous subject.

"There was a friend of mine when I was a boy," he finally

said. "His name was Jamie Crouse. He claimed to have seen it."

"What were the circumstances?" Marcie asked.

"You can't take this too seriously. I mean we were a small group of boys of around the same age, and Jamie was kind of our leader. He was always willing to do the stuff the rest of us wouldn't, like take the family boat when his parents were away and race around those red buoys."

"Isn't that where the floating trees are?" said Amanda.

William nodded. "One morning in the summer when there was so much fog over the lake that you couldn't even see the buoys, Jamie bet me five dollars that he could go through them without hitting any. I didn't want to bet him, but he kept going on about it so finally I bet him a dollar. I couldn't really see what happened from the shore because of the fog, but one minute his boat engine was roaring along, then the next minute it made a screaming sound and just stopped."

"What did you do?" Marcie asked, a rapt expression on her face.

"I went home and got Mrs. Ames. Dad was at work. We took our boat out. You couldn't see more than three feet in front of you, but we kept searching. Finally we spotted Jamie clinging with his one good arm to a piece of the boat's hull. It turned out his other arm was broken. He had a big gash on his head. And he was doing something that I'd never seen him do before. He was crying. From the moment we got him on the boat—and he must have been in a lot of pain—he kept saying that he'd seen the monster. We thought he was just hysterical from the shock, and he'd get over it. But that's what he told the police, and that's what he told his parents. That's what he kept telling everyone."

"Of course, no one believed him," Amanda said.

"No. His father even offered to buy another boat if Jamie would just admit that he had hit a tree or one of the buoys. But Jamie wouldn't. After a while even the other kids started to avoid him because he wouldn't stop talking about it, and he got real angry if you acted like you didn't believe him. He began to get in a lot of fights. We all figured that the accident had made him a little crazy. One time when the two of us were alone, he asked me if I believed him. I said I did because he was my friend, but I really didn't."

"What happened to Jamie?" Marcie asked.

"I don't know. His family sold their cottage over the next winter, and I never saw him again." Will stared out across the lake. "But thinking back now I don't think Jamie was lying. He must have really believed that he saw the monster."

"Why do you say that?" asked Amanda.

"Well, Jamie really loved taking the boat out, and his father got a newer, faster one right at the end of the summer because he thought it would help Jamie get back to normal. But Jamie refused to even take a look at it. I was there at the time, and I've never seen anyone look so scared as Jamie did when his father tried to drag him down to the end of the dock." Will paused and shook his head. "I don't know what he really did see out there that day, but I'm convinced that he *thought* he saw the monster."

Chapter Eighteen

Nick and Amanda pulled out of the parking lot of the inn and turned left on the main street that went through the center of West Windham. The desk clerk had assured him that if he went a half mile and then made a left at the light, he'd find Zenko's funeral parlor two blocks along on his right.

"What's Marcie doing this afternoon?" Nick asked.

"Working on a few additions to her Monster of Lake Opal story," Amanda said. She had already told Krow about their meeting with Will at the lake. "Marcie's going to see if she can put in some of the story Will told us into the article. That would spice it up a lot. If we don't use names and keep it vague, we can get away with it. Marcie has a good sense of how far to go without making the whole thing sound too sensational."

"Too bad we don't have some new information to add to

the story of Larissa's murder," Nick said. He glanced over at Amanda and saw that her eyes were dancing with mischief. "C'mon, tell me. You look like the cat that's swallowed the canary."

Amanda then went on to tell Nick about the information Marcie had gotten on Kirk's relationship with Larissa.

"The chief won't be happy to hear about that," Nick said. "He'll have to let the Portland police know, and this could end up costing Kirk his job."

"Maybe he won't tell them if he doesn't think it's relevant to the case," said Amanda.

"You don't think it's relevant?"

"I don't see how it would give Kirk a motive to commit murder. Like I told Marcie, Larissa wasn't going to spill the beans to anyone about their affair. She'd be the big loser if Martin divorced her."

"I wonder if Larissa's relationship with Kirk was still going on at the time she died?"

"All Ben said is that he didn't see Kirk's car at the cottage after the summer. What are you getting at?"

"Well, we know that Larissa may have been having an affair with the golf pro at the country club within six months of her marriage to Martin."

"Okay, so?"

"That probably ended when the gossip began to get intense. What I'm wondering is whether she broke up with Kirk because she was afraid people were finding out about them."

"But so far the only one who knew about them was Ben. No one else has mentioned it."

"Do you think Will could have known about Kirk's

relationship with Larissa, since he has a place out at the lake?" Nick asked.

"Hard to tell," Amanda said. "He claims that he doesn't get up to the lake much during the day, even in the summer. But Bethany might have spotted something and told him. I'm not sure she could see enough from their house, but if she went out in a boat, maybe she could. If Will did know, however, don't you think he would have told you about it? After all, he brought up the golf pro story."

"I was thinking more about whether he might have told his father."

"Why would Martin believe that any more than the story that went around the country club?"

Nick shrugged. "The first piece of malicious gossip about your beautiful young wife, you might dismiss. A second story catches your attention and makes you wonder if you were a fool not to believe the first one. Martin might have spied on them over that summer and found out what was going on."

"If you're suggesting that he might have killed Larissa, then why wait until the fall? And why start up this whole séance thing trying to find the killer?"

"You're right. Hiring a medium certainly doesn't make any sense. Plus I don't think it was Martin Chastain that I was fighting with last night at the cemetery." Krow grinned. "If it was, then I desperately need to start getting back into shape."

"Is there anyone else in town who might have wanted to see Larissa dead?" Amanda asked.

"There might have been hundreds, but I think we can limit ourselves to the people at the séance. Unless somebody made a phone call that night that they're not telling us about."

"Martin said he didn't tell anyone until the next day. We should check with Will and Bethany on whether they told anyone that night."

"And Devlin told me he didn't mention it to anyone. What about Mrs. Ames?" Krow asked. "She might have given her son a call."

"Good point. Marcie was with Kirk part of the night, but he dropped her off back at the inn around nine. His mother could have called him after that. He would have had time to get over to the cemetery before those kids came along."

"Still, like we already agreed, Kirk really doesn't have much of a motive for killing Larissa."

Amanda nodded. "No, I hate to say this Nick, but I think Will Chastain is still the person with motive and opportunity. He had no alibi for the time Larissa was killed, and he had the motive of protecting his inheritance. He also knew about the clue in the coffin, and could easily have gone home to get chain cutters and gotten over to the cemetery that night. Could he have been the guy you fought with?"

"I suppose so. Will was always pretty athletic, and I know he still goes to a health club. But why kill Larissa if she wasn't going to have a child? Why not wait until the problem arose? With all the affairs she apparently was having, it would only be a matter of time before his father would find out about her."

Amanda glanced over at Nick's troubled face. It was clear that he didn't want Will to be guilty, and she had to admit that she had warmed to the diffident, reflective man during her brief conversation with him at the lake."

"Maybe Larissa's coffin will give us a new suspect," she said brightly.

"I really hope so," Nick replied.

They pulled up in front of a two-story brick building with a discreet sign on the front lawn that said *Zenko and Son Funeral Home*. Two police cars were in the parking lot, along with a couple of civilian vehicles. Amanda and Nick went up to the front door that seemed to open as if by magic to reveal a young man in a dark suit. He looked down at a clipboard.

"Ms. Vickers and Mr. Krow?"

They nodded.

"Go straight down the hall, please."

They entered a large room with a plush carpet that was clearly intended for wakes. Today there was no casket up in the front and instead of being in rows, the chairs were arranged around the edges of the room. Martin Chastain and Eric Devlin were sitting next to each other, talking quietly. Chief Toth was standing with another young man in the required dark suit that identified him as one of the mortuary personnel. When he saw Amanda and Nick enter, the chief ambled across the room with a somber expression on his face.

"We've got a problem," he announced. "There was a break-in here this morning right after Larissa Chastain's body was delivered."

"How did that happen?" asked Krow.

"Louis Zenko and one of his employees picked up the coffin at the cemetery at nine o'clock and delivered it back here. The employee left because he wasn't needed until the afternoon. A few minutes later Louis got a call from someone who wanted to talk to him about purchasing a coffin. The person claimed to be housebound and sounded really desperate, so Louis locked the place up and left. The address he was given was ten miles out in the country and turned out to be fictitious. When he returned at ten-thirty, he found one of the back windows had been pried open."

"He doesn't have an alarm system?" asked Krow.

"I guess not many people try to break into funeral homes," the chief said.

"Can we tell if the coffin was opened?"

"Louis says that it could have been. The body isn't as neat as when it left the funeral home for the mausoleum, but that might easily have happened in transit out to the mausoleum or back. And, of course, there's no way to be positive if anything is missing. Louis is looking the body over right now to see if he spots anything odd." The chief sighed. "How you can tell that with a body that's been dead for six months, beats me."

Martin Chastain walked across the room toward them. He seemed more stooped than usual, and Amanda thought he looked ten years older than when she had seen him only yesterday. Edward Devlin trailed along behind him with a worried expression on his face.

"You have to catch the person who did this," Chastain said. "It must be the same man who killed my wife attempting to conceal his identity by destroying the clue Mrs. Narapov was talking about."

"We'll see," the chief said soothingly. "Louis is checking now to see if there's anything missing from the coffin."

"Why should he remember what was in there? Larissa was one of a hundred burials for him that year. I'm the only person who can tell for sure if anything is missing."

"And you'll have an opportunity to see the body, if you

wish to do so, once Zenko is finished with his examination," the chief promised.

"Why don't you sit down now, Martin?" Devlin said, taking the older man's arm.

Martin pulled his arm away petulantly. "I'm fine. And I intend to get to the bottom of this."

As if on cue, a middle-aged man in a dark suit came out from the back room.

"That's the undertaker, Louis Zenko," the chief said softly to Amanda and Nick.

Martin Chastain marched over to him, leaving Devlin behind.

"What did you find, Louis?" he demanded loudly.

The man smiled in a doleful manner that was probably meant to be soothing, but it seemed to anger Chastain even more.

"Well?" the older man shouted impatiently.

The undertaker blinked in surprise as though shocked by such rudeness in his place of business, but his expression instantly became more alert.

"I removed the body from the coffin and examined it carefully. It doesn't seem to have been interfered with in any way. I also removed the lining and thoroughly searched the inside of the coffin. I found nothing unexpected."

"I want to see my wife's body for myself," Chastain said in a tone that implied his serious doubts with regard to the undertaker's abilities to see the end of his own nose.

"Of course, of course."

Martin Chastain brushed past him toward the back room. Eric Devlin paused for a moment, as if wondering whether he was needed, then he hurried along, trying to catch up.

Louis Zenko walked over to Amanda and Nick and began to shepherd them toward the back room.

"We may as well all go in at once," he said, as if escorting people into the theatre. When he saw Amanda hold back, he took her arm in a firm grasp and smiled, "There's nothing too shocking for you to see, miss, but if you wish to wait out here . . ."

Deciding that this was the kind of man whose idea of fun in grade school had been to dangle worms in front of the little girls, Amanda knew that she had to rise to the challenge. She pulled away from Zenko's hand and took Nick's arm. They followed the others down a short hall into the back room.

"This is the preparation room," Zenko announced proudly.

To Amanda it appeared to be a cross between a commercial kitchen and a chemistry laboratory. Two gleaming steel tables connected to sinks dominated the center of the room. The walls were lined with shelves filled with brown bottles of chemicals. A pumplike machine on wheels stood ready to be rolled up to either table. The only unpleasant aspect was a smell in the air of what Amanda imagined must be embalming fluid. She knew she'd have to take a long hot shower tonight to get rid of the aroma.

She observed all this while walking across the room to join the others who had gathered around the table where the coffin rested. Forcing herself not to draw back, she moved with false eagerness to look down at the center of attraction.

Zenko had been right, there was little to be shocked about. The woman lying nestled in the bed of silk appeared to be sleeping, sleeping a bit rigidly, to be sure, with her lips tightly closed together and her hands folded rigidly across her chest. Her features were regular, even attractive, although Amanda suspected that much of Larissa's charm had come from her animated expressions, which were gone forever. All that betrayed her current state were blotches of colorings ranging from darker brown to tan on various parts of her face, as if she had gone to sleep in the act of trying out different shades of cosmetics.

"She still looks beautiful," Devlin said, then blushed as though embarrassed by the stupidity of his comment.

"Thank you," Zenko said proudly, not embarrassed at all. "Good embalming can often delay any sign of decomposition for a long period of time."

"Decomposition can also be delayed by environmental factors as well, can't it?" Krow asked.

"Of course," the undertaker said, warming to the subject. "Sandy soil or a dry tomb can cause desiccation. A dried-out body will look rather leathery but not show much decay at all. Even in very wet conditions *adipocere* may develop as the body's fat forms what in the old days they called grave wax due to the breakdown of the fat into fatty acids. Such corpses often look quite lifelike. Perhaps that's the origin of the 'undead' among superstitious peoples."

The chief cleared his throat. "Maybe we should get back to the business at hand."

"Sorry, chief," Krow said.

Martin Chastain had ignored the conversation around him, intently studying his wife's corpse as if trying to detect any sign of life. His left ear was bent down close to her lips. Amanda wondered a bit giddily if he expected Larissa to whisper the name of her murderer to him.

"Does everything look the same?" the chief asked, then realizing that the question was open to interpretation, he hurried on to say, "I mean, are any items missing or have any been added?"

Chastain continued staring for a moment as if he hadn't heard the question, then he slowly shook his head in disappointment. "Everything appears the same."

Amanda forced herself to take a closer look at the corpse. Larissa was wearing a dark red dress that might have been considered by some to be a bit festive for the occasion, but it worked well with her blond hair. *Probably chosen by Mrs. Ames,* Amanda thought. Around her neck she wore the turquoise locket the housekeeper had told her about when they were examining the holdings of Larissa's closet. She wore her engagement ring and wedding ring on her left hand.

"You found nothing out of the ordinary," the chief said to Zenko.

The undertaker shook his head.

"And there's no sign that anything had been removed from the coffin?"

The man cleared his throat. "There was no evidence of that. But since the coffin was not sealed, there is no way for me to know with certainty if any unauthorized parties have had access to Mrs. Chastain since her entombment."

The chief gave the undertaker a searching look, then turned to Chastain.

"Well, sir, I'm afraid that there's nothing here to help with the investigation into your wife's death."

Chastain glanced up with a puzzled expression as if not quite understanding what was being said, then he slowly reached down to his wife's chest and picked up the locket that lay between her breasts. He snapped the locket open. Everyone leaned forward expectantly, but all they saw were facing photographs of Larissa and Martin.

"Oh, Larissa," Martin said softly.

The chief glanced at Krow and Devlin, silently asking for help.

"Martin, I think that either we misinterpreted what was said at the séance or else someone got to the clue before us," Nick said.

The man nodded dumbly, appearing to be in shock.

"Why don't we go somewhere else to discuss this?" Eric Devlin suggested with a note of urgency in his voice as he took Chastain's arm.

Devlin was looking a bit uncomfortable, and Amanda had to admit that the smells and the presence of the body were beginning to bother her as well. She hoped a new location also might bring Martin back to his senses.

"Will I be able to see her again?" Martin asked the undertaker.

"Of course. We won't be returning the coffin to the mausoleum before tomorrow. If you'd like to go into the next room while I straighten up here."

Everyone except for the undertaker returned to the room they had first been in. Devlin and Krow arranged some chairs in a circle, and they sat in what seemed to Amanda like mimicry of a séance.

"What do we do next?" Martin asked in a lost voice.

Nothing was said for a moment. Amanda thought that everyone realized that Martin had expected the viewing to provide clear evidence of the identity of his wife's murderer, and without that, he had suddenly been cut adrift. But at the same time, no one seemed sure what to suggest as the next course of action.

"Why don't we return to where we started?" Nick finally said in a businesslike tone. "Is Mrs. Narapov still in town?"

Martin nodded his head. "She's staying at the inn. But she plans to leave today."

"Well, maybe we can catch her before she leaves and have her conduct another séance."

"What would be the purpose in that?" Martin asked doubtfully. "It doesn't seem as though the last one did us much good."

"Possibly we misinterpreted the information that Larissa provided and another séance would give us further clarification. Or possibly the clue was stolen."

"Don't you think that one séance has caused everyone enough trouble?" the chief said sharply. "That led to a boy being almost killed and you being attacked. Who knows what this woman will say the next time? Plus we've still got a killer around here who takes this stuff seriously. Another false clue would just open the door to more trouble."

"I agree," Devlin said, echoing the police chief.

"But it also might lead to the killer's revealing himself," Krow pointed out. "There may have been a valuable clue in the coffin that he stole this morning, but even if there wasn't, the killer can't assume that the next message won't be accurate. He'll be forced into action, which will make it more likely that he'll be caught."

"This case was pretty much closed until Mrs. Narapov's prediction," Amanda added. "What do we have to lose?"

The chief sighed and looked over at Martin. "I can't order you to hold another séance. The decision is yours."

"I'll talk to Mrs. Narapov and see if she would be willing to contact Larissa again," Martin said. Suddenly he sat up straighter and seemed to pull himself together by an effort of will. "I also think that it's time for me to recognize that I can't continue on this way forever. I'm going to go through all of Larissa's things very carefully and dispose of them. I've kept her personal effects exactly as they were on the day she died, but now it's time to accept the fact that she's gone."

His voice trembled on the last word, as if accepting that fact was something he was struggling to do.

"There's no rush," Amanda said softly.

Martin looked up at her and smiled faintly. "Thank you, my dear, but it is time. I'll get Mrs. Ames to help me. Larissa had so many clothes, plus she had duplicates of almost all her jewelry. We should go over each piece before deciding what to do with it."

"Good idea," the chief said in a bracing tone that was clearly meant to get Martin back on a more positive track.

"Why don't we go now, Martin?" Eric Devlin said, taking him by the elbow and helping him to his feet.

"One more thing," Martin said. "I don't want Larissa returned to that mausoleum. It's not safe. It's bad enough that she was murdered, I won't have her coffin violated again. I'm going to speak with Louis about having her body cremated once the next séance is completed. Given her fear about being buried alive, it's what I should have done from the first."

"That's a big decision," Eric said hesitantly.

"And it's one I'm ready to make."

The strength of his voice was undercut by the shakiness of his steps as Eric helped him across the room. Amanda felt that everyone was as surprised as she was by how quickly the vigorous man in his sixties had seemed to decline, although his rally at the end had been impressive. Having staked so much on finding a clue in Larissa's coffin, it was natural that his disappointment was serving to magnify his sense of loss. She thought, not for the first time, that becoming so emotionally attached to another person could have devastating consequences. Perhaps it was better to remain alone and suffer occasional loneliness than to leave oneself open to this type of emotional injury.

The chief, Nick, and Amanda stayed behind as if by unspoken agreement and watched as the other two men made their way out the front door. After the door was closed by one of the employees, the three looked at each other.

"Were Larissa's letters and e-mails checked by the Portland police?" Krow asked.

The chief nodded. "Even though they thought it was a mugging, they went over everything in case she had received any threats or strange messages that she hadn't mentioned to her husband. There was nothing suspicious. I doubt that Martin will find anything helpful by going through her personal effects."

"Just a sense of closure," Amanda said.

"We did find out something you should know," Krow said, glancing at Amanda for permission and seeing her nod. "Ben told Marcie that Kirk Ames was having an affair with Larissa Chastain."

The chief's watery blue eyes opened wide for a moment then became narrow slits.

"Damn that fool," he muttered. "I knew that boy was too good-looking for his own good."

"It may not have anything to do with the murder."

"Still, now I've got to decide whether to tell the boys in Portland about it. Kirk should have come to me about this himself as soon as the murder happened. Keeping it secret like this makes him look bad."

"It's your call, chief," Nick said. "We aren't going to tell anyone. But maybe you could find out from Kirk whether he was still seeing Larissa at the time of her death."

"And could you find out if his mother called him the night of the séance, and told him Mrs. Narapov's message?" Amanda asked.

The chief gave a curt nod. "Don't worry, I'll run his sorry ass through a wringer until I find out every detail. Do you really think that another séance is going to help us any?"

"To be honest, I couldn't think of anything else to suggest," Nick replied. "Like I said, the killer took the last one so seriously, I thought another one might bring him out in the open again."

"So you'll both be staying in town until we find out if and when another séance can be arranged?"

"I can manage one more day," Krow said.

The chief turned to Amanda, "How about you?"

"I really shouldn't," she said. Then another of the recent recurring waves of irresponsibility swept over her. "But I'm sure that I can rearrange my schedule."

Chapter Nineteen

Marcie walked out of her room and stood for a moment, looking down the hall. When the woman working on the reception desk had discovered why Marcie was in town, she had proudly mentioned that the inn had its very own ghost. Reportedly it was the spirit of an elderly man who had stayed in a room on the third floor back in the late eighteen hundreds. He had been traveling through the area and had died suddenly, probably of a stroke, leaving no papers by which he could be identified. Over the years various guests and members of the staff had reported being approached by a man with gray hair and long mutton-chop sideburns, dressed in an odd black suit. He would ask them "to tell Charlotte that I'm here." The figure was described as having an ethereal, transparent quality, and when the listener drew closer, he would slowly vanish.

The woman had offered to put Marcie on the third floor

where all of the sightings of the apparition had taken place. She had declined, firmly deciding that it was one thing to deal with the supernatural during the business day but another to have to confront them on your own time. She knew that with her imagination, once she turned out the lights every dark corner would turn into a human figure and whispered Charlottes would fill the air.

But as Marcie stood in the hallway, which was always dark because only a small, drapery-covered window at the end of the hall provided any light, she was suddenly tempted to go up to the third floor just to see if something ghostly would appear. Her bravery was due to feeling satisfied with herself for having completed a draft of what she considered to be a more than adequate article on the Monster of Lake Opal, and Marcie figured that maybe she owed herself a little illicit excitement.

As she paused, trying to arrive at a decision, she heard a door down the hall behind her open. She turned and saw a dark figure approaching her, blotting out the faint light from the window. Marcie stared hard where the figure's face would be, hoping to pierce the shadows and see what she was confronting. Only when the figure was almost on top of her did she realize that rather than being the ghost of a long dead old man, it was actually a very much alive Mrs. Narapov.

"Don't you know it's not polite to stare?" the woman said, brushing roughly past her in the narrow hallway.

A flash of anger overcame Marcie. "Going to see if they found a clue in Larissa's coffin or whether you've been revealed as a fraud?" she shot back.

The woman turned slowly. The light from the window

down at the end of the hall caught her full in the face and seemed to magically intensify her features. The malicious smile on the woman's face frightened Marcie, and she immediately regretted her comment.

"That wasn't what you thought the other day, little girl. Who was that I heard from in the spirit world? Your dead mommy or grammy."

Marcie's stomach tightened, and she had to force out the words. "You didn't hear from anyone in the spirit world the other day, and you never have."

"Don't be so sure of that."

The woman's eyes locked onto Marcie's and in an instant she was floating, drifting off down the shadowy hallway toward some unnamed horror. Then Marcie closed her eyes and felt the floor come back under her feet again. When she found the courage to open her eyes again, Narapov had disappeared. Marcie leaned against the wall thinking to herself that all she needed right now was to run into an old guy mumbling "Charlotte." Fortunately, no one else came down the hall, so a moment later after composing herself, she went down the stairs into the lobby, just as Amanda and Nick entered.

"Are you okay?" Amanda asked, giving her an appraising look.

"Yeah. I just had a short conversation with Mrs. Narapov, everyone's favorite medium."

"We saw her too." Nick said. "We told her that nothing was found in Larissa's casket and that Martin Chastain would be wanting to talk to her about holding another séance. She said that he'd just called her on her cell phone, and she was on her way up to his house. She didn't look very happy about it."

"So there wasn't anything in the coffin?" Marcie said with a smile of triumph. "So I guess Narapov is just an old fraud."

"Maybe," Amanda said, and nodded toward the empty room off to the side of the main hallway. "Why don't we talk about it in there?"

They all went into the dark parlor and sat in the corner farthest from the front door. Marcie ended up on the horse-hair sofa, which seemed kind of prickly. It also didn't make it easy to move around since her corduroys seemed to form a tight bond with the sofa seat.

"So what happened?" Marcie asked, the excitement obvious on her face. "Did you actually see Larissa's body?"

Nick and Amanda took turns explaining what had happened at the funeral parlor. When they were finished, Marcie told them about her brief encounter with Mrs. Narapov in the hallway.

"That woman is a witch," Marcie concluded.

"I think the word begins with a *b*," Amanda said dryly. "I wonder how she'll respond to our not finding anything in the coffin?"

Nick shrugged. "She can always claim that the guy who broke in took it. I'm more interested in finding out whether she'll be willing to do another séance with Larissa so soon."

"Does it bother the dead to be contacted too many times in a week?" Marcie asked.

"Some mediums would say that," Nick replied with a smile at the earnestness of the question. "But the more supposed contact we have with Larissa, the harder it is for Mrs. Narapov to make vague predictions. We're putting her on the spot to be more and more specific. I wouldn't be surprised if she refuses."

"She might go along with it if Martin insists," Amanda said. "After all, she's probably been hoping to have a lucrative long-term relationship with him."

"So Mr. Chastain was really upset that you didn't find anything in the coffin?" asked Marcie.

Amanda nodded. "It seems to have finally hit home with him that Larissa isn't coming back. He's even talking about sorting through her things and having her body cremated."

Marcie shook her head.

"What the matter?" Nick asked.

"It's just that he sounds like such a conservative guy, and she must have been pretty weird."

"You mean because of her affairs?" asked Nick.

"Actually, I was thinking more of her being in the cemetery at night."

Amanda and Nick stared hard at her.

Marcie caught their expressions of surprise and blushed. "Did I forget to tell you about that?"

"Why don't you tell us about it now," Nick said softly, barely concealing the annoyance in his voice.

"Sorry. Ben mentioned it at the same time he told me that Kirk was having an affair with Larissa. I guess the stuff about Kirk made me forget about the other thing."

"Which was?" Nick persisted.

"Just what I said. Ben used to see Larissa walking through the cemetery after dark."

"When was this?" asked Amanda.

"Ben said it started at the end of last summer and continued until right before she died."

"Did he know where she was going?"

Marcie shook her head. "Ben asked her once, and she told him to mind his own business."

Nick slowly rocked the foot that was crossed over his knee up and down as he stared across the room.

"Let's assume she left from her house. Where would she be going if she walked through the cemetery?"

"That would be the most direct way downtown," Amanda answered. "It would also be a route that would keep her out of sight of anyone driving on the road."

"So if she wanted to go somewhere downtown after dark without being seen, that would be the best route," Nick said slowly. "Mrs. Ames told you that Martin Chastain frequently worked at night, so if Larissa wanted to meet up with someone in secret maybe that would be how she'd do it. If Martin did come home and wonder where she had been, Larissa could always claim that she'd just gone out for a walk."

"The timing works too," Marcie said in an excited voice. "Ben said that Kirk stopped showing up at the lake house right around the end of the summer, so maybe Larissa found a new boyfriend right about then."

"One who lived downtown," Amanda said.

"And everything was fine until Ben spotted her going through the cemetery," Marcie continued.

Amanda turned toward Marcie.

"A couple of days ago you said something about the possibility that Larissa might have been getting together with Kirk in Portland."

"Yeah. I said that maybe they had a fight, and he killed her in a hotel room."

"Well, what if you were partly right. What if Larissa

decided that Ben was getting too nosy about her trips through the cemetery, so she decided to start seeing her new boyfriend in Portland? And what if they got into a fight, and the guy followed her as she went back to her car and killed her."

"There's a lot of 'what ifs' there," Nick said.

"But it would explain why the killer would be someone who knew about the séance. It's because he's someone right here in town, but he was meeting up with Larissa in Portland."

Nick took out his cell phone. "I'm going to give the chief a call and see what he thinks of our idea. Maybe he could get the Portland police to show Larissa's photo around hotels in the area where her body was found."

When Nick walked off to a far corner of the room, Amanda studied Marcie, who was slumped on the sofa staring at her scuffed running shoes.

"What's the matter?"

Her friend shrugged. "Guess I'm still a little bummed about Kirk. He seemed like a nice guy at first. Maybe a little too stuck on himself and being macho cop, but nothing really bad. Finding out about him and Larissa is making me wonder whether I understand men at all."

"Give it time," Amanda said, smiling to herself at the world-weary sound of Marcie's remark. "You don't have that much experience."

"Will it get easier when I do?"

"Understanding men is the easy part," Amanda replied.

"What's the hard part?"

"Understanding yourself."

Nick returned and checked his watch. "Well, the chief is

going to give it some thought, but I wouldn't hold my breath. He hasn't brought Portland into the case yet, and I don't think he's likely to unless we come up with some hard evidence. I don't think he wants the guys in the big city to know that he's chasing down a lead from a ghost. I'm off to see Will Chastain. I promised to fill him in on what happened at the mortician's. Not that what I have to tell him will be of much help."

"Find out if he told anyone about what happened at the séance on the night that it took place," said Amanda. "Maybe that will give us another suspect to add to our list."

"Right now I'd like to narrow the list down to the one who actually did it," Nick said. "Are you two free for dinner tonight? I was thinking of going out to see what culinary delights West Windham has to offer in the evening."

Marcie declined, saying that she was planning to have a light supper and get some reading done in her room. In reality she would have enjoyed nothing more than going with them, but she knew that Nick was only inviting her to be polite. Just because her budding friendship with Kirk had hit a brick wall was no reason for her to horn in on whatever Amanda and Nick had going.

"Are you sure you won't come along?" Nick asked her.

The obvious sincerity of the offer touched Marcie, but she remained firm.

He turned to Amanda. "How about we meet in the lobby around seven?"

Amanda nodded. When Nick had left, Amanda said, "Are you sure you won't join us? You won't be in the way. We probably aren't going to talk about anything more personal than who killed Larissa Chastain."

"Maybe you should," Marcie said, immediately wishing she could take back the words. "Sorry, none of my business."

"You like Nick, don't you?"

Marcie nodded.

"So do I, but I'm just not sure—"

"What you're going to do about Jeff."

"Exactly."

Marcie slid awkwardly off the sofa, her corduroys sticking like glue and making a loud rubbing sound.

"Well, I'm tired of thinking about men. And I'm tired of thinking about Larissa Chastain, the Monster of Lake Opal, and pretty much everything having to do with this town. That's why I think a quiet night alone is just what the doctor ordered."

Amanda smiled. "Enjoy it. And maybe tomorrow will be our last day here."

"I sincerely hope so," Marcie replied.

Chapter Twenty

I have done all that I can do. I got the mortician out of the building, so I could examine Larissa's coffin. Poor Larissa! When I was there alone with her and held her cold hand for a moment, I told her how sorry I was that she had died. And how important to me was the time that we had spent together.

But that's in the past. All I can do now is to try to save myself. When I found nothing in her coffin that could do me any harm, I was confused. I was sure I knew what the clue was. Had the medium been wrong? Was the whole thing a cheap fraud from start to finish? But, no, I think I understand. The medium said that spirits often answer questions indirectly. Now I know where the clue is, and it is still a danger to me. I must retrieve it quickly or all will be lost. There is great risk, but it is a risk that must be taken for my future and to protect Larissa's memory.

Chapter Twenty-one

Nick had never seen Will look quite so forlorn. Even after they had lost the soccer conference championship back in '95, Will had been the only guy on the team who seemed to keep his sense of balance. Although Nick hadn't appreciated Will's comment as they walked back to the dorm that it was only a game, by the next day when he was able to see things more objectively, Nick had found the statement to be remarkable mature. Now as Nick studied his friend from across the restaurant where they had eaten before, he suddenly realized that Will hadn't been mature at all. The reason why he could remain so dispassionate about losing the championship is that nothing had ever mattered very much to him except to have the love and respect of his father. His father hadn't cared about his playing soccer, so Will had never invested much emotion in the outcome.

As Nick crossed the room and settled in across the table from his friend, Will looked up and managed a thin smile. A waitress hurried over and they both ordered coffee.

"So what did you find?" Will asked after the coffee arrived.

While Nick described the events at the mortuary, Will's face showed no emotion except for slight surprise when Nick told how his father had decided to get rid of Larissa's things and order her cremation.

"So there was no clue after all," he said flatly after Nick was done.

"Unless the intruder took it."

"And do you think my dad was serious about putting Larissa behind him?"

Nick shrugged. "He seemed to be."

"Good. Maybe that will put an end to his fascination with the supernatural at the same time."

"Well, there's something else I have to tell you," Nick began hesitantly. "I suggested that we have another séance."

"*You* suggested that? Why?"

"Larissa's killer is still out there, and he's somebody local. Somebody who found out about what happened at the first séance and got worried enough to break into the mausoleum and the mortuary. You don't want that person hovering around your family, do you?"

The appeal to the safety of his family seemed to work, because Will shook his head.

"You're right, of course, if Larissa wasn't killed in a random mugging, then we have to catch the murderer. But do you really think another séance will help?"

"For some reason the killer seems to believe Narapov's

messages, so maybe he can be provoked to come out into the open once again. By the way, did you tell anyone that night about what was said at the séance?"

"No. Bethany and I went straight home, and we didn't call anyone." He paused, lost in thought. "Too bad we can't get Narapov to make up a message that would help us to catch the killer."

Nick considered the idea, then shook his head. "Mrs. Narapov isn't the most amenable of people, and she'd probably see it as a request that she violate her professional ethics."

Will snorted. "I'd hardly consider it a profession."

"There's something else I've found out that you should know about. There's some evidence that Larissa was having an affair with Kirk Ames during the summer just before her death."

"The deputy?"

"Ben saw Kirk's car up at your father's lake cottage a number of times during July and August."

A disgusted look passed over Will's face. "I knew she was a tramp, but I just can't believe she'd do that to my father."

"Do what?"

"Carry on with someone right at Dad's place. In fact I can't believe that Kirk would do it. His mother is practically a member of the family."

"So you didn't know anything about this?"

"How would I?"

"Since Bethany and the kids spent so much time up at the lake during the summer, I wondered if she might have noticed something and mentioned it to you."

"And then I went out and killed Larissa?" Will paused and

looked out the restaurant window. "Maybe I would have if I'd known."

"But you didn't know?"

Will shook his head. "If you'd ever been out to Lake Opal, you'd realize that you can't see Dad's place very clearly from where I live. Maybe if you were out in a boat you could, but Bethany is deathly afraid of the water. I'm the one who takes the kids out, and that's in the evening after I get home from work."

"Ben also said that in the fall he frequently saw Larissa walking through the cemetery at night. Do you have any idea where she would have been going?"

"No. Larissa and I occasionally went to charity events together in the evening to represent the company, but otherwise, I had no idea what she was up to at night."

"Why did you and Larissa go to those things together? I can't imagine that you enjoyed being with her."

Will smiled grimly. "I hated it, but it was my small sacrifice for the business. Dad would rather stay late at work, or if he did come home, he'd stay in his study reading some technical journal. He's never been much for small talk, and he couldn't be bothered helping to promote the company in the community."

"Why didn't you take Bethany to these events? She could have gone along with you and Larissa."

"She doesn't like large groups. She's happiest at home taking care of the children."

"Didn't you tell me once that she was an elementary school teacher when you met her?"

"That's right. She taught second grade. One of the little boys in her class had lost a leg in a car accident, and she asked the company to send someone to explain to the other children how a prosthetic limb worked. She thought it would make the boy's transition back to school easier. That's how we met."

"I'll bet she's wonderful with children."

Will's face clouded over. "I think she was happiest working at the school. She's rather shy around adults, but really comes out of herself when she's around children. I don't know what we'll do when ours are off to school. She won't know what to do with her time. Maybe she'll go back to teaching again."

"So you have no idea where Larissa might have been heading when she cut across the cemetery?" Nick asked, returning to the subject.

"None at all. But from what you've been telling me, she was probably meeting some man."

"That's what I wondered. Do you know where Kirk Ames lives?"

"His mother told me once: a condominium about two miles outside of town. Too far for Larissa to easily walk, especially at night. And the cemetery would be in the wrong direction."

"Maybe she was seeing someone else. Did you ever notice Larissa paying particular attention to anyone at the gatherings you attended with her?"

"I'm afraid that I thought she was coming on to every man she met. A lot of it might have been harmless flirting. Dad was probably right about that. It was her way. But I couldn't tell you what was serious and what wasn't."

"Did she ever show any interest in you?"

A look of disgust passed over Will's face. "No, thank

God. One thing Larissa and I agreed on is that we really didn't like each other. Even if she had never met my dad, we wouldn't have hit it off. She was everything I didn't like in a woman, and I'm sure she thought that I was too weak and passive to be a real man."

"What about Eric Devlin? She must have seen quite a bit of him."

"I think Eric was the one person that Larissa may have been a little jealous of because he's so close to my father. Eric and I talked about Larissa right after Dad married her, and we both agreed that all we could do was let her relationship with Dad run its course. We both hoped that eventually Dad would see through her and get a divorce."

"Looks like that would have happened sooner rather than later given Larissa's behavior."

"But somebody killed her first," Will said staring down at the table. "You know, it would have been better for Dad if they had gotten a divorce. He'd have been pretty cut up for a while, but at least he'd have seen her for what she was and eventually gotten over it. By getting murdered, she'll always stay in his mind as this passionate woman who loved him. He'll probably never recover from that."

"Well, he is having her body cremated," Nick said. "That's a beginning."

"Too bad he can't burn her out of his mind as easily."

Chapter Twenty-two

Marcie put her book on the table next to the bed. It was a collection of folk stories about supernatural happenings in New England. Amanda had read up on this kind of thing for several months before starting the "Weird Happenings" column, and Marcie had been trying to get up to speed since she had begun working on the magazine.

The number and variety of tales that had sprung up from colonial times to the present was amazing. Marcie could certainly understand how the first settlers, clinging to the coast by the skin of their teeth and confronted by a vast, dark wilderness, might had imagined all sorts of things, but that people today could be adding to that folklore really fascinated her. Although she might not have readily admitted it, Marcie was pleased that she was making her own contribution to that tradition.

She rolled off the bed, did a back bend to work out the

kinks, then walked over to the window. It was getting dark outside. She checked her watch and saw that it was 5:00. She'd spotted a deli around the corner from the inn that had a tempting array of meats and cheeses in its case and advertised overstuffed sandwiches. Marcie did some mental negotiations with herself and decided that she could afford to have the calories in half a sandwich if she substituted a garden salad for the other half. She'd grab a soda to go with it and eat in her room. A small table next to the single chair could serve as a dining table.

Marcie went down the hall, relieved that she didn't run into Mrs. Narapov again. *It was amazing how some people just have your number,* she thought, *and no matter how hard you try to resist, they can get under your skin.* Narapov had that effect on her, and Marcie imagined that she would be a pain in the neck to a lot of people. Several people were already seated in the dining room as she walked past and out the front door, and the traffic on the main street was as busy as it got in West Windham, a steady flow with no slowdowns.

She had just turned the corner to head down to the deli when someone grabbed her shoulder from behind and spun her around.

"I was just coming to see you," Kirk said, squeezing her left arm hard. "I wanted to know what I ever did to you that you'd want to screw up my life."

"What are you talking about?" Marcie asked, furiously twisting out of his grasp. That was the way her father had always grabbed her when he was getting ready to toss her in the closet for the punishment of some fictitious wrong. *No one was ever going to touch me that way again,* she thought, bunching up her fists.

The expression on her face made Kirk pause for an instant, but then his own anger drove him forward.

"The chief said that Ben saw me out at the Chastain cottage that summer. The only person Ben would ever have told about that is you. I want to know why you ratted me out."

"We're in the middle of a murder investigation," Marcie said, trying to maintain a reasonable tone of voice. "We have to look at all the men who were involved with Larissa because one of them may be the murderer."

"So it's not enough that I might lose my job, now you're trying to get me sent to prison for murder," Kirk said with a bitter laugh.

Marcie glanced up the street behind Kirk. It was amazing how suddenly a street in the middle of town could empty out. There was one woman on the next block walking toward them. Marcie wondered if she could rush past Kirk and reach the woman before he caught her. But what would that accomplish? Kirk was in uniform, and the woman would be more likely to believe him than a young woman trying to tell a complicated story.

"Nobody's trying to send you to prison," she said sharply, deciding that appearing unafraid was her best hope. "And if you end up there, or if you lose your job, it will be your own fault, not mine. You're the one who got involved with a married woman and didn't tell anyone after she was murdered."

Kirk's normally handsome face twisted into a grimace of pain. "And what do you think would have happened if I had admitted everything to the chief six months ago? He'd have told the Portland police, and I'd probably be standing trial right now."

"For a cop you don't have much confidence in the system. Were you still seeing Larissa at the time of her death?"

"No. We broke up three months before."

"Why?"

A flash of pain passed over Kirk's face. "She said she'd met someone else."

"Who?"

"She wouldn't tell me."

"Were you in Portland the day Larissa was murdered?"

"No. But I did have the day off."

"What did you do?"

Kirk shrugged. "Hung around my place. Went to the supermarket for food. Stopped by the Chastain house to see my mom."

"So you have witnesses who can account for your whereabouts for at least part of the time. Why are you so worried?"

Kirk took a deep breath and the anger seemed to drain from his face.

"Ever since Larissa died I've been a wreck. Chief Toth is strict. If I admitted to him that I'd been having an affair with a married woman, that alone might be enough to destroy my career. Plus the Portland police really wanted to solve this one because Martin Chastain is an important guy, so I knew that if they found out about me, it would be like waving red meat in front of a hungry lion. Who knows if my alibi would be really watertight? Larissa and I really tried to keep things secret, so I figured that no one knew about us. It seemed safer just to say nothing."

Marcie reached out and touched his arm. "I can understand that. Sometimes it's hard to tell the truth when it doesn't seem absolutely necessary."

Kirk nodded. "Looking back I can see that was a mistake. What I feel worse about is that the chief has been good to me and I didn't come clean with him. Now he'll look bad."

"Have you told him that?"

"He didn't give me a chance to say much of anything. He just asked me a few questions and once he found out that I'd been with Larissa, he suspended me."

"He's upset too. Give it a little time. Then go and apologize to him. Maybe there's still some hope for your career."

"Yeah. I guess I'll give that a try. I just came from telling my mom. I don't know what's going to happen to her. She might even lose her job when Mr. Chastain finds out."

"She's worked there for a long time. He can't blame her for something that was . . ."

"My fault," Kirk said. "Well, you never know."

"What I don't understand is how you let yourself get involved with Larissa in the first place."

"I'm not sure I know why either. We met one day when she locked herself out of her car by the city hall." He smiled and shook his head. "There was just something about her. I knew all the time I was seeing her that it was stupid and wrong, but it was like quicksand—the more I struggled, the deeper I sank."

"You should have grabbed a branch and pulled yourself out."

"I suppose." He gave Marcie a long look. "What about us? Is there still a chance for us to get together?"

Marcie didn't know whether to laugh or cry at the fact that Kirk would ask such a question in the midst of a life that was falling down around his ears. A horde of questions rushed through her mind. She seized the one that seemed most important.

"Why did you ask me out in the first place? Were you bored because Larissa wasn't around anymore? Were you ready to make your next conquest?" Kirk took a step backwards and shook his head.

"I really cared for Larissa. I know that sounds kind of weird considering that she was another man's wife, but I did, and I thought she felt the same way about me." He smiled to himself sadly. "I guess Larissa was good at making men think that. Anyway, when she walked out, she pretty much said that I was just some guy who kept her amused for a little while."

Marcie liked him better now that the arrogance was gone, but her expression remained neutral.

"That got me to look at my life, and I started thinking that I wasn't much better than she was. Most of my relationships have been just for fun, and I know that I've hurt a lot of people along the way. I decided that wasn't what I wanted anymore. When I met you, I thought that maybe this was my chance to begin over again."

Marcie could appreciate Kirk's change of heart, but she warned herself to be cautious, not to be taken in by his plea for understanding.

"So will you give me another chance? That's all I'm asking."

"Why don't we wait until we see how all of this works out." she replied. "You've got a lot of other things to worry about right now."

Kirk nodded sadly, then turned and walked away.

"This seems like a nice place," Amanda said, placing her menu to one side and glancing around the room.

Although the ceilings soared up at least fourteen feet high to scarred wooden beams that along with the wide plank floors revealed the building's origins as a mill, the dark wood paneling and the dim lighting softened the atmosphere to something more suitable for a restaurant.

"Hard to imagine that a hundred years ago people toiled away in here for twelve hours a day," Nick said.

Amanda shook her head. "Be careful or I'll feel too guilty to eat."

"If we did, Mrs. Narapov would tell us that the spirits of those who suffered over the mechanical looms still permeate the building and are haunting us."

"Do you think that's true?"

"That buildings hold the emotions of former inhabitants?" Nick shrugged. "I've read a lot of pseudo-scientific stuff about energy lingering at the scene of traumatic events. As far as I know, physicists would discount the whole idea."

"Still, it's an idea that makes some sense, even if physicists can't explain it."

"Sure, and let's not give scientists too much credit. A lot of them believe in life after death, even though their science would argue against it. Most people are pretty good at using logic to destroy the other guy's point of view, but are pretty reluctant to use it on their own pet theories."

"Is that what Martin Chastain is doing?"

"I think so, at least up until today. Not finding a clue in the casket seems to have been a watershed event for him. It's brought him down to earth, and now he's ready to get on with his life."

"Maybe," Amanda said, taking a sip of water.

"You think he'll revert back to his enthusiasm for the supernatural?"

"I don't know. It just seemed so sudden. I guess I would have expected a man who's been as successful in life as Martin has been to be a bit more determined to pursue a path once he's started along it."

"You mean he should have been more willing to hold a second séance?"

Amanda nodded. "He just seemed ready to give up too easily."

"My theory is that he was never really wholly committed to this supernatural approach to things. Probably Mrs. Narapov had done a pretty good job convincing him to give it a try, but it was just a working hypothesis for him. Once it didn't pan out he was ready to abandon it."

"That makes sense," Amanda admitted as their waitress stopped at the table to take their order. When she walked away, Amanda gave Nick a mischievous smile. "Don't think I've forgotten about that explanation you owe me."

"Explanation of what?"

"How you got to be a private consultant for the Portland police."

Nick smiled. "Ah, that story. Well, there isn't much to tell. It started with a family that claimed they had a poltergeist. Things were flying around their house, and they kept calling the police. Finally a friend of mine on the force asked if I had any suggestions as to how to put an end to it. With the father of the family's permission, I went in and installed some small surveillance cameras in the rooms where most of the action had taken place." Nick paused and looked expectantly at Amanda.

"Did they have a teenaged daughter?" she asked.

"I see you have been reading up. She was fourteen years old and very good. When everyone in the room was looking the other way, she would throw an object across the room and return to the most normal posture you can imagine almost instantly. We had it all on tape. Another paranormal phenomenon disproved."

"Some researchers think that teenaged girls have so much pent-up emotion that it comes out in the form of moving things with their minds. Do you think that's possible?"

"Psychokinesis? Lots of claims but little evidence. Some scientists think it's possible, others don't. I'd have to see it to believe it."

"You really are a skeptic."

"Aren't you? Surely you aren't looking for weird things to happen just for the thrill of it like Marcie."

"No. I wouldn't go that far. But I guess I find the possibility of supernatural events kind of intriguing."

"It makes for good stories, but encourages a lot of illogical thinking."

Amanda sighed. "I guess there are occasions—rare I'll admit—when I feel that logic is overrated."

Nick was silent for a moment, then he asked, "So are you still seeing that lawyer in Portland? What's his name? Jeff?"

Amanda nodded, thinking that Nick's recall of Jeff's

name, which she had only mentioned once almost six months ago, showed that he was more interested in her than she had thought.

"Do the two of you have any plans for the future?"

"You mean like having dinner together next week?" Amanda asked.

"Okay, point taken. I'm being too nosy."

Amanda looked across the room and Nick watched her carefully, waiting for her to make up her mind about how much to tell him.

"As a matter of fact," Amanda said, "Jeff has a new job and is moving to the Washington, D.C., area."

Nick tried unsuccessfully to keep his face from brightening.

"He's asked me to go with him."

"Are you going to?" Nick asked heavily.

"I've spent the last few days trying to decide."

"That sort of answers the question then, doesn't it."

"What do you mean?"

"Well, if I asked a girl to move in with me and it took her a week or more to decide, I think I'd rescind my offer."

"Why?"

Nick gave a short laugh. "Don't you think it shows a striking lack of enthusiasm?"

"But it's such a big decision."

"It shouldn't be. You've been going out with this guy for how long?"

"About eight months."

"That's long enough for you to have answered all the big questions already. Didn't you ever consider that this relationship might move on to the next step, maybe even marriage?"

The blank expression of Amanda's face told him the answer.

"You sound like you're standing up for Jeff and that my taking so long to make a decision is somehow unfair. Is this some kind of male bonding thing?"

Nick grinned. "Hey, don't misunderstand me. I'm thrilled that you aren't planning to run off with Jeff, but I just don't understand how you can go out with a guy for so long and not consider it any kind of commitment."

"Well, Jeff never said anything," Amanda said defensively.

"Men don't. But I'll bet he was assuming a whole lot."

"Then he assumed wrong," Amanda replied shortly. "And before you start saying anything about my unwillingness to make a commitment, let me point out that I don't see a ring on your finger. Have you ever been married or even engaged?"

Nick's expression turned serious. "I was engaged once, but she was killed in an automobile accident."

Amanda felt herself blush with embarrassment. She reached across the table and touched the back of Nick's hand. "I'm sorry. I didn't know."

"Yeah, well it was quite a while ago now—almost eight years. That's how I first got interested in this paranormal psychology stuff. One of her roommates wanted to hold a séance, and she asked me to attend. It was the most blatant hoax I'd ever seen, really took advantage of our feelings of loss. It made me determined to expose this kind of fraud whenever it occurred."

"You haven't been seriously involved with anyone since then?"

Nick shrugged. "It took me a while to start dating again after Sarah's death. I guess being with her gave me pretty high standards because no one has come close, at least until recently."

Nick looked into Amanda's eyes. She held his glance for a moment, then stared down at the table.

"I guess you're right, I don't have as good an excuse for being commitment-shy as you do. But we can't help being the way we are."

"Maybe that isn't your problem at all. It could be that you just knew that Jeff wasn't the right guy for you."

To Amanda's relief the waitress arrived at the table with their food before she had to respond.

Chapter Twenty-three

*N*o television! Marcie thought angrily for the tenth time that night. The country charm that the West Windham Inn boasted of so proudly purposely excluded any sort of modern technology, so the only item in the room that wouldn't have been there in the nineteenth century was a clock radio. Marcie had already exhausted that as a source of interest, and after reading until her eyes began to blur, she was at loose ends for something to do.

Now that she had eaten her sandwich and salad, it seemed to Marcie that the room smelled like a deli that had failed its sanitation inspection. She bounced off the bed, walked across the room, and tried to open the room's one window. But the lock had been painted over so many times that she couldn't twist it open. Since the inn did have air conditioning—wonder of wonders—it was possible that no one had tried to open the window in a number of years.

Apparently the only way to escape from the smell of her own overindulgence was to leave the room. But where to go was the question. A stroll around downtown West Windham after dark didn't have much appeal, but Marcie decided that a short walk up and down the main strip would at least clear her head and help to work off some of the calories she had consumed.

She pulled on her coat and went out into the hall, closing the door behind her. She paused a moment, debating whether she should take her gloves. Although she could always shove her hands in her pockets, she had read somewhere that it burned more calories if you were able to swing your arms freely. Hunting around in her coat pocket for the key to get back into her room, she turned away from the stairs and glanced up the hall. The dimly lit hall seemed brighter than usual, and a second later it registered with Marcie that the source of the light was coming from the room three doors up. The door was open, and as Marcie watched, a figure came stumbling out into the hall and quickly headed toward her, bouncing wildly off the walls like a billiard ball.

Drunk, Marcie thought, quickly pulling out her key and getting ready to rush back into her room to avoid a potentially awkward encounter. The door to her room was open when she risked a glance back at the figure that had now stopped and was leaning against the wall several yards away breathing heavily and moaning. The light from the room hit her face and Marcie recognized Mrs. Narapov.

"Are you all right?" Marcie asked, cautiously moving closer, wondering whether the woman was ill or having a powerful supernatural experience.

Mrs. Narapov pushed herself off the wall and stared directly at Marcie. A look of recognition slowly came over her face. She stared into Marcie's eyes.

"A fraud! All a fraud!" she shouted, and before Marcie could ask what she meant, the woman fell face down in the center of the hall with a sickening thud.

"Is she dead?" Marcie asked.

She was back sitting on the wretched horsehair sofa in the front room of the West Windham Inn again. The waitress from the bar had insisted that she take a glass of brandy. After one taste, which was enough to tell her that it resembled medicine more than refreshment, Marcie had sat there with the glass clutched in her hand as if it would calm her down by mere proximity. Now she was looking over at Nick, Amanda, and Chief Toth. The chief had arrived right after the EMTs who had been called when Marcie had rushed downstairs to report Mrs. Narapov's collapse at the front desk. Amanda and Nick had arrived back from dinner five minutes later. Amanda had stayed with Marcie, while Nick and the chief went upstairs.

"She probably died almost immediately after she collapsed," the chief answered softly. "Someone had hit her very hard on the back of the head."

"I didn't see anyone leave the room right before she staggered out."

Chief Toth adjusted his large body in the upholstered chair that had sunk down nearly to the floor under his weight.

"We think that she may have been hit a few minutes before you saw her. There's a small puddle of blood on the floor in her room. She was probably lying there for a few minutes, then regained consciousness and staggered out into the hall looking for help. We'll know more once the state forensic unit has a chance to examine the scene. We've already questioned the staff and those who were in their rooms at the time. Nobody saw anything unusual."

"And I almost went scurrying back into my room, thinking she was drunk," Marcie said.

"She was already a dead woman," the chief said. "We won't be sure until the autopsy, but a blow like that would have caused so much immediate damage that her brain was already swelling with blood. It was a miracle that she ever made it back on her feet."

"Too bad she didn't tell me who attacked her," Marcie said.

"Tell me what she said again."

Marcie repeated Mrs. Narapov's last words.

"I wonder what she meant?" Amanda said.

"Maybe she was just admitting that she was a fraud," the chief suggested. "A sort of deathbed confession."

Amanda shook her head. "The woman had just made this superhuman effort to get out into the hall and then she sees Marcie, someone she knows. I think she'd try to say something more directly related to her attacker."

"She could have been referring to another person, saying that someone else is a fraud," Nick said.

"Wrong noun," Amanda pointed out. "If she'd said 'he's a fraud' that would make sense. But 'all a fraud' suggests she was talking about something else."

"Maybe this whole business with Larissa Chastain's ghost," the chief said hopefully. "I wouldn't mind finding out that business was all a scam."

"We should talk to Martin Chastain," Nick suggested. "He met with Mrs. Narapov a couple of hours ago. Maybe he can give us some suggestions about what she was trying to say."

The chief nodded. With an audible grunt he heaved himself out of the collapsed chair and took his cell phone off his belt. "I'll give Chastain a call and find out if he can see us tonight."

Amanda, Nick, and Marcie sat in silence for a moment after the chief walked out into the hall. Marcie was staring at the rug as if trying to decipher a message hidden in the faded pattern. Nick gave Amanda a look that seemed to be urging her to say something.

"Are you sure you're all right, Marcie?" Amanda asked. "If you're not comfortable staying here tonight, we can leave now and be home in a little over an hour. I'm sure the chief would give us permission."

Marcie looked up. Her expression was bland and unfocused, but as Amanda watched she saw firmness and determination return to her face.

"I wasn't that happy about hanging around here in the first place, but now I've got a reason to want to see it through. I really want to find out who did that to Mrs. Narapov."

"You don't have any responsibility to her," Nick pointed out. "You didn't even like her."

"Doesn't matter," Marcie snapped. "Someone hit her over the head and left her to die, and I saw it. I take that personally."

Nick paused for a moment, then smiled. "Yeah, I can see that," he said admiringly. "Good for you."

Amanda looked from one to the other. "This must be some kind of competitive jock thing that you two have in common. All I'm saying is that if you want to leave, I'm more than willing to go with you right now."

"How much longer can we stay?" Marcie asked.

"I've already gotten Greg's permission to stay through tomorrow, and since tomorrow is Friday, I guess we can hang around until Sunday if we have to."

"Good," Marcie said.

Chief Toth came back into the room and stood at the end of the sofa.

"Mr. Chastain has agreed to see us right away. He seemed very upset to hear about Mrs. Narapov's death."

"That's natural if he considered her his one remaining link with Larissa," Nick observed.

The chief nodded and looked over at Amanda and Nick. "I'd like you to go with me again."

"What about me?" Marcie asked.

"I don't want to turn this into a parade," the chief said. "Martin doesn't know you, and I'm not sure that this is the right time to get another civilian involved in the investigation."

Marcie opened her mouth to object, but Amanda said, "Don't worry. We'll fill you in on everything we find out. You've had a bad shock. It might be just as well if you got some rest. We can talk about everything tomorrow over breakfast."

Marcie felt her mouth tighten in anger at being patronized, but a wave of bone-deep weariness swept over her and suddenly she felt as if the trip up the stairs to her room was almost more than she could manage.

"Okay," she said, struggling to her feet. She walked to the end of the sofa and carefully set the half-full glass of brandy down on an end table, then she leaned on the sofa for a moment to get her balance. "But we *will* talk about it in the morning."

Amanda nodded and watched carefully as her friend carefully made her way out of the room.

"Will she be all right?" Nick asked. "Maybe you should go with her to her room."

"I think she'll be all right, but I'll check on her in a couple of minutes before we leave to go to Mr. Chastain's," Amanda said.

"Is there any particular line of questioning you're going to pursue with Martin?" Nick asked the chief.

"Nothing fancy. I'm just going to ask him what he talked about with the woman and find out if she said anything about meeting with someone else."

"You could have done that over the phone," Nick pointed out.

"Sure. But then I couldn't see his eyes."

"You don't think of him as a suspect, do you?" Amanda asked.

"Everyone involved in this case is a suspect, as far as I'm concerned. Almost anyone could have killed Larissa Chastain and the same goes for the Narapov woman."

"Don't you trust us?" Amanda asked with an innocent smile.

"Not completely. But I don't think any of you three could have been Larissa's murderer, and that puts you halfway in the clear." The chief turned toward the door that had suddenly filled with men in state police uniforms. "Now why don't you two get your coats and meet me down here in the lobby in ten minutes. I'll drive."

"Do you really think that the chief doesn't fully trust us?" Amanda asked Nick as they walked up the stairs to their rooms.

"Since he found out about Kirk, I'm not sure how much he trusts himself."

Chapter Twenty-four

M rs. Ames opened the door and wordlessly motioned for them to enter the hallway. Amanda gave her a small smile, but it was greeted with a stony expression that suggested the woman was blaming all three of them for the misfortune that had befallen her son. "It was his own fault," Amanda was tempted to tell her, but she knew that would only be pouring gasoline on the flames. A suitcase was on the floor next to the door. Chief Toth looked at it thoughtfully for a moment.

Mrs. Ames stood in front of them, blocking their way into the living room.

"I haven't told him about my son and Larissa," she said to the chief. "I was hoping that it wouldn't be necessary."

"I don't know yet," the chief said, holding her gaze. "It's too soon to tell."

She nodded and went back down the hall to the kitchen.

208

Martin Chastain and Eric Devlin were sitting in front of the fireplace with drinks in their hands. Martin stood up quickly when he saw his guests enter and went to the door-way to escort them into the room. Amanda thought he seemed livelier than he had earlier in the day.

"What a terrible thing! Do you have any idea what happened?" he asked the chief.

"Someone hit her on the head," was the blunt reply.

Toth's eyes were fixed on Chastain as if trying to ascertain whether there was a guilty reaction. But Martin merely shook his head as if mystified by the increasing level of violence in the world.

"That's horrible," he said, glancing over at Eric Devlin, who had a suitably somber expression. "But please sit down. I'll certainly help you in any way I can."

The chief took out his notebook. "What time did you see Mrs. Narapov?"

"It was around seven. Right after dinner. I'd invited her to come to dinner, but she declined."

"How long was she here?"

"Approximately fifteen minutes."

"How did she get here?"

"She walked. I offered to drive her back to the inn, but she refused. She said it had only taken her about twenty minutes to make the walk, and that she enjoyed walking at night."

"You spoke to her about conducting another séance?" the chief asked.

Martin rubbed his hand slowly along the arm of the sofa. "She was quite upset that we hadn't found anything more significant in Larissa's coffin. I tried to tell her that it was no reflection on her abilities. After all, there had been an intruder in the mortuary, so the clue could have been stolen. Or perhaps Larissa herself wasn't quite clear in what she wanted to communicate. However, I'm afraid that nothing I said did much to soothe her. She was very upset because she thought this event might damage her reputation."

"There must have been numerous times in the past when her predictions didn't come true," said Krow. "Why was this particular one be so upsetting to her?"

"I gather it was because it was related to a murder case. Mrs. Narapov felt that she had gone out on a limb with a clear prediction, and so it was particularly upsetting when it couldn't be confirmed. She believed that when word got out about this she would be considered a fraud. I told her that I would do everything in my power to see that her reputation would come out of this untarnished, but she didn't seem to believe that was possible."

"Was she willing to conduct another séance or not?" asked the chief.

Martin shook his head. "I asked her to, but she refused. Mrs. Narapov said that the vibrations emanating from Larissa were clearly unreliable, and she wasn't willing to risk another false prediction."

"And she left around seven-thirty?" asked the chief, making a note.

Chastain nodded.

"Were you here for that conversation?" Nick asked Eric Devlin.

"No, I only arrived about fifteen minutes ago. Martin called me when he heard about Mrs. Narapov's death, and I offered to come over."

"Are you a lawyer?" the chief asked.

"No, a financial consultant," Devlin replied, slightly startled.

"Do I need a lawyer?" Martin Chastain asked with a smile.

The chief shook his head. "So far I haven't got any suspects."

"I didn't stand to gain anything by Mrs. Narapov's death," Martin said, then he looked across the room and it seemed to Amanda that his eyes filmed over with tears. "In fact her death deprived me of my only means of communicating with my wife."

"Did she discuss anything else with you while she was here?" the chief asked.

Martin nodded. "Another reason why Mrs. Narapov was reluctant to conduct another séance was that she'd had a vision. She was concerned that the spiritual energy she was tapping into was becoming too strong."

"What kind of a vision?" Nick asked, suddenly interested.

"She said that the recurring image of a chain kept forming in her mind."

"What type of a chain?"

Martin shrugged. "She didn't know. All she said was that she kept seeing the links of a chain. Apparently the details were fuzzy. She had no sense of its size or length."

"And she was disturbed by this image?" Amanda asked.

"She seemed to think that it was connected to Larissa's death in some way. But I also believe that she was concerned because of the power of the vision. It kept occurring to her without warning and was beyond her control. For all of her willingness to contact the other side, Mrs. Narapov was the kind who liked to contact the spirit world on her own terms."

Controlled contacts with the supernatural. Amanda thought that seemed a bit like being a moderate heroin user: something easier to wish for than to realize.

"So you were alone with her during this conversation?" the chief asked.

Martin nodded.

"And where were you for the next hour or so?"

"Right here in the house."

"Can anyone confirm that?"

"No. Mrs. Ames went to her son's place for dinner. She left some dinner for me and only arrived back here twenty minutes ago to clean up."

"So she must have arrived shortly before you did, Mr. Devlin?" the chief asked.

The man nodded. "She came into the living room and told us she was back. That was about five minutes after I arrived."

"And where were you when Mr. Chastain called you?" the chief asked, looking down at his notebook and preparing to write.

"Me?" Devlin paused for a moment as if the question presented unusual challenges. "I was at my office downtown."

"On Main Street?"

Devlin nodded.

"About how far from the West Windham Inn?"

"Two blocks."

"And you were in your office when Mr. Chastain called you?"

"That's right."

"Can you confirm that, sir?" the chief asked Martin.

"I'm afraid I can't," Martin said, giving Devlin an apologetic look. "I called him on his cell phone, not on the office land line."

"Were you in the West Windham Inn at anytime this afternoon or evening?" the chief asked the younger man.

Devlin shook his head. "I haven't been inside the inn for weeks."

"Had you met with Mrs. Narapov at any time since the séance?"

"No."

The chief glanced at Amanda and Nick to see if they had any further questions, then climbed to his feet.

"I may have some more questions for both of you gentlemen. But that's all for right now." Martin Chastain accompanied them out into the hall where the chief looked again at the suitcase.

"Are you planning a trip?"

"I'm going to spend the next few nights up at the lake cottage. Mrs. Ames and I began going through Larissa's things today, so my bedroom is quite a mess."

"Let me know if you find anything that might help with the case," the chief said.

"Of course."

They were putting their coats on in the vestibule when Martin Chastain spoke.

"Was a chain in any way used in the attack on my wife?"

"It isn't mentioned in the police reports," the chief replied.

Martin gazed up the dark staircase, as if hoping to see Larissa come waltzing down to greet him.

"I know it sounds silly, but could you double check on that for me? Mrs. Narapov seemed so certain that her vision was connected with my wife's death that I'd like to be certain."

"I'll get in touch with the Portland PD tomorrow morning."

"Thank you."

They were riding back to town in the cruiser when the chief spoke.

"So what did you make out of all that?" he asked. Receiving no response, he glanced in the rearview mirror at Amanda.

"Neither one of them have alibis for the time of Mrs. Narapov's death," she answered. "But I don't see why Chastain would want her dead, she was his only avenue of communication with Larissa, and I don't see how Eric Devlin comes into this at all."

The chief nodded. "But his having an office only a couple of blocks from the inn is certainly convenient." He waited a moment then glanced over at Krow, who was staring out the window. "What about you, any thoughts?"

"I'm wondering why Mrs. Narapov would have been having a vision of a chain."

The chief nodded. "Yeah. I can't figure out how that relates to the case either. I'm pretty positive there was no chain involved in the attack on Larissa."

"It's just odd that she would have that sort of vision."

"What are you getting at?" Amanda asked, leaning forward from the back seat.

"Mediums like Mrs. Narapov are usually consistent. If they get verbal cues, then those are the kind they get. After all, she talks to spirits in the next world and they speak to her, so language is usually involved. For a medium like that to suddenly start having pictorial visions without words—well, it's very uncommon. Some mediums do get mostly visualizations, but very few receive both."

"So do you think Narapov was lying?" the chief asked. "Maybe she'd just come up with a new way to play her con on Chastain."

Krow shrugged. "I can't see why she would, when the old one seemed to be working. And I also don't know why she would pass on this visualization to Martin if she was unwilling to hold another séance. Why dangle this new clue in front of him, then refuse to try to find out what it means by contacting the other side?"

"Maybe she was holding out for more money?" the chief suggested.

"I suppose that's always possible," Krow replied doubtfully.

"What are you going to do next?" Amanda asked the chief.

"Would you be willing to come along with me to see William Chastain and his wife? I gave them a call earlier, and they agreed to talk with me."

"How would Will be connected to Mrs. Narapov's death?" Nick asked.

"I don't know that he is, but I want to talk to everyone who was at that séance. Plus William Chastain wasn't real keen on having his father talking with Larissa's ghost."

"That doesn't mean he'd kill her," Nick said.

"I realize that." The chief paused. "I understand that William is an old friend, so if you'd rather not be along when I talk to him I can always go myself, or maybe Ms. Vickers would be willing to come along."

Krow pressed his lips together. "No, I'll come along and I'll behave myself."

Chapter Twenty-five

William Chastain opened the front door. He ran a hand across his forehead, then struggled to paste a polite smile on his face.

"Come on in," he offered in a voice that sounded weary.

"Sorry to bother you," the chief said. "I realize it's late to be disturbing a family with young children."

On cue the sound of children's voices came echoing down the stairway from the second floor.

"My wife will be down in a minute. She's just putting the children to bed."

They made a left into the living room. Amanda was amused to see that both in style and decoration the house was a slightly smaller version of the senior Chastain's. Given that Will's taste in architecture ran to the more contemporary, Amanda wondered whether this reflected Bethany's influence.

"Have you lived here long?" she asked Will.

He nodded. "From when we first got married. Dad gave it to us as a wedding present."

So the modern house on Lake Opal was a later rebellion, Amanda thought.

"It's not exactly to my taste anymore," William said, confirming her suspicions. "But it's the only home the boys have known, and we don't really have any compelling reason to move."

When they were all seated and had refused the offer of something to drink, the chief slowly cleared his throat and pulled out his notebook.

"Can you tell us where you were between seven-thirty and eight-thirty this evening?"

A look of concern passed over William's face and he opened his mouth as if about to ask whether he was a suspect in Mrs. Narapov's death. Then the triteness of the question and the inevitably evasive reply seemed to play out for him in his mind and he nodded.

"I got home from work at nine o'clock."

"Is that the normal time?" the chief asked.

He gave a choked laugh in response. "My wife would say that there is no normal, and I suppose she's right. I come home when the work is done and that varies. But usually I'm home by seven."

"So you were delayed tonight?"

"I had to prepare a presentation for tomorrow and some of the materials I needed arrived late."

"What time did you leave work?"

"Eight-fifteen or thereabouts. It usually takes me half an hour to get home, but I stopped for gas."

"Can anyone at work confirm that time?"

"No. Pretty much everyone else had left for the night. One of the cleaning staff might have seen me. I'm not sure."

Bethany Chastain slipped into the room. She settled on the edge of a chair in the corner, as if hoping to avoid attention.

"Were you aware that your father planned to ask Mrs. Narapov to conduct a second séance?" the chief asked.

William nodded. "Nick had told me earlier. I saw Dad at work late this afternoon and told him in no uncertain terms that I thought it was a terrible idea. I'm afraid that we argued about it."

"You didn't like the idea of another séance?"

"I didn't like the idea of the first one," William snapped.

"What about you, Bethany?" Amanda asked. "What did you think about the plans for another séance?"

"I didn't know about it until Will came home." She paused as if hoping that much of an answer would be adequate, but the expectant expression on Amanda's face forced her to go on. "I can understand why Martin might want to find out who murdered Larissa. But I think that he should leave it to the police."

The bland expression on Bethany's face bothered Amanda.

"What was your opinion of Larissa Chastain?" she asked.

Bethany looked shocked. "I . . . I didn't have much to do with her."

Amanda looked incredulous. "She was your stepmother-in-law."

"Well, of course, I saw her at family gatherings."

"Do you think she planned to have a child with Martin?"

Out of the corner of her eye, Amanda saw Will give a start as if he wanted to intervene.

Bethany's mouth twisted in a bitter smile. "She told me she did. Larissa said that she wanted to make sure that at least some of Martin's money went to a child he had by her."

"How did you feel about that?" Amanda asked.

"Will is Martin's son," Bethany said, speaking very fast and fixing her eyes on her husband. "He's helped his father all his life. We deserve whatever Martin leaves behind. For Larissa it was just some kind of a game. A way for her to prove that she was the most important person in Martin's life. She was an evil person, and I'm glad that she's dead."

Bethany collapsed back into the chair and looked down at her hands contritely as if she expected to be punished for expressing such a childish opinion. Will went over and stood beside her.

"Do you have a car?"

Bethany nodded.

"Where were you from seven-thirty to eight-thirty?" the chief asked.

"Right here," she replied, calm again.

"Is there anyone that can confirm that?"

She nodded. "My children."

Nick glanced across at Amanda. She could see that he was thinking the same thing she was. That no one had a good alibi for the time of Mrs. Narapov's death.

"Any one of the four could have killed Narapov, none of them had an alibi worth squat," the chief blurted out in exasperation as they headed back to the inn.

"Which four are you talking about?" asked Amanda.

"Martin and Will Chastain, Bethany Chastain, and Eric Devlin. Any one of them could have been in Narapov's room between seven-thirty and eight-thirty."

"So which one of them killed Larissa Chastain?" Amanda asked softly. "It would have to be the same person who killed Larissa if we assume that Mrs. Narapov was murdered because she was going to supply another clue."

"But she refused to hold another séance," the chief pointed out.

"According to Martin," Nick said softly.

He'd remained quiet while they were at William Chastain's. His only comments had been a brief "hello" and "goodbye" to Will. Amanda had suspected that he didn't want to antagonize his friend more than necessary.

"Martin and William don't have alibis for the time of Larissa's death," the chief said. "The Portland police probably didn't check out Bethany, and they wouldn't have known anything about Eric Devlin."

"So that doesn't help us to eliminate any suspects?" Krow said.

"What if we assume that the person who attacked you in the cemetery is also the same person who killed Larissa and Mrs. Narapov," Amanda said to Nick. "Wouldn't that eliminate Bethany and Martin?"

"Which leaves us with William Chastain and Eric Devlin as our primary suspects," Chief Toth concluded with a note of triumph. "Good work, Amanda, now we're getting somewhere."

"And since Eric had no motive for killing Larissa as far as we know . . ." Amanda said reluctantly.

"Will is still our primary suspect," Nick concluded with a grimace.

"Money and the love of his father are powerful motives. And from what Bethany just said, it sounds like Larissa was going to try to take away both of them," the chief said. "Even if Will didn't want to kill Larissa, his wife may have pressured him into it."

Nick waved a despairing hand but said nothing.

The chief's face took on a more determined look. "I'm going to have my people show William's picture around downtown tomorrow morning. We have one in the Portland file. I'd like to know if he was near the inn this evening. He glanced over at Nick. "Sorry this isn't working out better for you."

Nick smiled faintly. "I don't blame you, chief. You're just following the evidence."

"But I'll tell you what I'll do. I'll also have my guys check to see if anyone saw Eric Devlin around the inn tonight."

"Thanks. I appreciate that," Nick replied.

"And we shouldn't leave out Kirk Ames," Amanda said from the back seat. "When I went up to look in on Marcie just before we left, she said that Kirk had talked to her on the street outside the inn a couple of hours before the murder."

"Why did he do that?" the chief snapped.

"Apparently he blamed her for being suspended."

"That damned fool will get himself thrown off the force yet," the chief said, reddening. "I told him to stay away from everyone involved with the case."

"And he was Larissa's lover, so he does have a possible motive for killing her," Amanda continued.

"But he told me that they broke up a couple of months

before her death," the chief objected. "She took up with a new guy."

"It wouldn't be the first time a jilted lover decided that if he couldn't have her nobody would," Amanda pointed out.

"Okay, okay" the chief relented. "I'll show a picture of Kirk around too. May as well make sure that he didn't go into the inn tonight."

"Sounds like we've still got too many suspects," Amanda said from the back seat.

Neither of the men responded.

"Feel like having a drink?" Nick asked Amanda as they entered the lobby of the inn.

Normally Amanda would have declined. She didn't drink when she was tired because it seemed too much like using alcohol as a kind of crutch. The way her father had used it to ward off his dark moods. But she knew that Nick wanted to talk.

"Okay," she said. "Just give me a minute to check my voice mail. I'll meet you in the bar. Order a glass of chardonnay for me, would you?"

She stepped into the room off the lobby where the three of them seemed to spend so much of their time. Amanda smiled to herself as she wondered whether the room had gotten as much use in the last decade as it had in the last week. She perched on the edge of a straight-backed chair. Her smiled faded as she listened to her first voice mail.

"Hi . . . this is Jeff. It's Friday, and as I hope you remember, I'll be leaving on Sunday to drive down to Washington. Things are kind of a mess as you can imagine. Everything is sort of half packed. Anyway, I called you at work and they told me you were away on an assignment. I know you said that you needed some time to decide whether to come down to Washington with me. It's been almost a week . . . I guess I didn't figure it would take you this long to make up your mind—maybe I should figure that not getting back to me is your decision. Anyway, I'm leaving Monday morning. If I don't hear anything by Sunday, well good luck, and it's been fun."

Amanda sank back in the wooden chair. The hard back hit her painfully across the shoulders as though punishing her for not having been more forthright with Jeff. It wasn't like her to avoid making decisions, especially the difficult ones. *So why am I fumbling this one so badly?* Staring across the shadowy room that was lit only by two table lamps in the far corners, she realized that it wasn't because she didn't like Jeff. She did, probably more than any other man she'd dated. But was it love? How much *like* did you have to have before it turned into *love?* Amanda wondered. Or maybe one never became the other because they were on completely different dimensions.

The other problem was that for the first time she could remember, she was happy with her life. *Roaming New England* magazine had given her the one thing she'd never had before, a sense of being part of a small, reasonably happy family. Her biological family had never provided that, and despite all the excitement of working on a newspaper in Boston, there she had always felt herself to be in competition with those around her rather than part of a team. Although she had always been critical of people who settled into nice comfortable jobs rather than constantly pushing to go further, she was beginning to see the benefits of having a niche. To give all that up to go live with Jeff seemed to be too much of a sacrifice.

But a little voice warned her, when it came to work, nothing lasted very long. What if Greg left as general editor and was replaced by some harridan? Amanda knew then that she'd be out looking for a new job by the end of the month. Was it foolish of her to give up a chance of personal happiness with Jeff just because she liked her present working situation?

"Problems?" Nick asked as she settled into the booth across from him.

"Aren't there always?" Amanda replied, taking a sip of her wine.

Nick waited for her to continue, but when Amanda gave him one of her practiced polite smiles, he realized that she wasn't going to be any more forthcoming.

Amanda glanced at Nick's glass of beer. "I'm surprised to see you with beer. The other night weren't you touting the virtues of single malt scotch?"

Nick grinned. "I think better with a beer. It brings me back to my working-class roots."

"Ah, the academic working class. Has the beer helped you come up with any good ideas?"

"Not really. But I'm still not feeling right about this whole thing."

"There's no reason why you should. An old friend the main suspect in a murder, and we still don't have much to go on."

Krow nodded absentmindedly.

"Is there something else that's bothering you?"

He shrugged. "I guess it all goes back to the séance. The way Mrs. Narapov came up with that business about the clue in the coffin. I still can't get over how direct and clear that was. It almost seemed like it was staged."

"I thought these séances were all staged," Amanda said with a smile.

"Yes. But like I've been saying over and over again, usually the medium is more speculative. Their predictions have more qualifiers than a drug advertisement. And now there's this business about the chain. That just doesn't sound like something that Mrs. Narapov would say either."

"What are you suggesting? Do you think that she had some agenda of her own? If she was working with Larissa's killer, I doubt that she'd have been giving hints about where incriminating evidence was hidden. In fact I don't see how it would benefit the killer at all to have a séance conducted."

Krow ran his hands through his hair. "I know. That's why I think we're looking at this from the wrong angle. If we could just shift our perspective a bit, I think everything would fall into place."

"Well, I've always found that you can't force that sort of thing. If it happens, it happens suddenly. And the best thing for it is a good night's sleep, which is exactly what I think I'm going to get," she said.

"Have you decided yet about whether you're going to move to Washington?"

She gave irritated frown.

Nick smiled. "Maybe a good night's sleep will help with that too."

Chapter Twenty-six

Nick rolled over and made a grab in the general direction of the ringing phone. He knocked his watch and keys onto the carpeted floor before his hand closed around the smooth handset.

"Hello?"

"This is Chief Toth. Are you awake enough to understand me, Krow?"

"Sure," Nick half-lied.

"Eric Devlin has been shot to death."

"Another murder?"

"Not exactly. I'll explain it to you when you get here. I'm at Martin Chastain's house."

"I'm on my way," Nick said, managing to swing his legs over the side of the bed.

"Is Ms. Vickers there by any chance?"

"It's three in the morning, chief," Krow pointed out.

"I know. I just thought that maybe . . ."

"I'm not that lucky," Nick said with all the honesty of the half-awake.

The chief chuckled. "Well, it's up to you if you want to call her or come alone. But since you've both been in on it from the start, I'd like to have at least one of you here to help me question Chastain."

"Yeah, okay," Nick said, hanging up. He rubbed a hand over his face and wondered whether it would be better to let Amanda sleep. But then he imagined the look on her face the next morning when she discovered that he'd left her out of the investigation. That convinced him to give her a call.

"So what's going on?" Amanda asked him a fast fifteen minutes later, as they met in the lobby of the inn.

"Don't know, other than that Devlin's been killed."

Krow looked at Amanda who had pulled her hair back into a ponytail and wasn't wearing make-up. Her face still softened by sleep made her appear younger and more vulnerable, and a strong desire to hold her in his arms swept over him.

"What's the matter?" she asked, eyeing him suspiciously.

"Not a thing," he replied, opening the door to the outside. A blast of cold air forced instant wakefulness.

When they reached the Chastain house, a deputy silently motioned them into the living room. Martin Chastain was on the same spot where he had been seated the night before. Across from him were the chief and a young deputy who had his notebook out and looked nervously alert.

The chief nodded and motioned for Amanda to sit on the opposite end of the sofa from Chastain. Nick drew up an occasional chair from the corner of the room and placed it next to the deputy.

"I'm glad you're here. Mr. Chastain was just going to go over what happened one more time for the record," the chief said and gave Chastain a nod that he should begin.

"Like I said before, I don't know how long I'd been asleep, but I awoke suddenly. I looked at the clock and saw that it was three o'clock. I turned over to go back to sleep when I heard a noise in what's usually my bedroom."

"Where were you sleeping?" the chief asked.

"The guest room across the hall."

"I thought you were going to spend the night at the lake house?" Nick asked. "That's what you told us when we were here earlier."

"That's what I had planned to do, but I started to do some work after Eric left. By the time I was done it was nearly eleven, and I didn't feel like making the drive out there. The bed in the guest room was already made up, so I just used that."

"Let's backtrack a minute," the chief suggested. "At what time did Eric Devlin leave?"

"He didn't stay long after you left. Actually he seemed to suddenly be in quite a hurry. He mentioned something about wanting to go back to his office for awhile before going home. I guess he left at around nine."

"Was Mrs. Ames here when he left?" the chief asked.

Martin nodded. "She left about fifteen minutes later."

"And then you worked until eleven."

"That's right."

"But when Devlin left he would have been under the impression that you were going to spend the night at the lake."

"Yes. I suppose so."

"Okay. So you woke up at three and heard a noise in what is usually your bedroom. What happened next?"

"I just lay there for a while waiting to see if I heard the noise again. I've never had a break-in before so I thought I was just imagining things."

"Do you have a security system?" asked Amanda.

"My first wife had one installed, but I haven't used it since her death. I'm not even sure whether it still works." Martin blinked slowly and peered across the large room. "I really don't keep much of value in the house."

"What happened next?" the chief asked.

"I lay there staring at the ceiling for a while, listening. Then I finally decided that I was never going to get back to sleep unless I checked out the noise. So I went across the hall and into my bedroom."

"Why didn't you call the police?" asked Amanda.

"I didn't know if anyone was really there." He smiled sheepishly. "I didn't want to look silly by crying wolf."

"Did you turn on the lights when you entered your bed-room?" the chief asked.

Martin shook his head. "I thought that if someone really was in there I might have the advantage if he didn't see me coming."

"So you slipped into the room in the dark."

"I stepped into the room and listened. It seemed like a sound might be coming from our dressing room, and I thought that I saw an occasional flash of light under the door. So I went across the room to my bedside table and took out the handgun I keep there." Martin looked up at the chief. "It's registered. I have another one at the lake house."

"You don't use your security system, but you keep a handgun by your bed?" asked the chief.

Martin sighed. "My first wife again. She insisted that I have it. She was a very nervous person at night."

"But you kept it in your bedside table for over twenty years after she died?"

"I really didn't know where else to put it. I felt it was safe because I never told anyone that it was there. I doubt that even Larissa knew about it. I would clean it and put in fresh ammunition about once a year. I even debated turning it in to the police because I had no use for it, but I never got around to it."

"Did Eric Devlin know you had a gun?'

"No."

"So you took out the gun, then what happened?"

"I really didn't know what to do. I was tempted to call the police, but I still wasn't completely convinced that someone was in there. When we'd had that dressing room built, Larissa had insisted that it be soundproofed. She liked to sleep late in the morning, whereas I get up at the crack of dawn to go to work. That way I wouldn't disturb her while I was getting ready," he explained.

"So you thought someone might be in the dressing room. What did you do next? Did you just stand there by the bed with a gun in your hand? Did you walk toward the door to the dressing room?"

Martin frowned. "I walked across the room and stood in between the door to the dressing room and the door to the bedroom." He gave an embarrassed smile. "I guess I couldn't decide whether to run out of the room or charge straight ahead and find out who was in there. "If I had done either one of those, then maybe Eric would still be alive."

"What happened next?"

"Well, I was standing there trying to decide what to do when the door opened and suddenly a flashlight was shining in my eyes. I was blinded. I called out . . . I think it was something like 'Stop or I'll shoot!' but I'm not completely sure."

"But the person kept coming."

"Yes, right toward me. I guess he was frantic, trying to get out of the room. Eric must not have realized that I was standing directly in front of him because he charged right toward me. I didn't know what to do, so I held the gun up with both hands and pulled the trigger twice. All I could think was that I had to stop the attacker. The sound deafened me, and I was stunned for several seconds. Finally I stumbled over to the wall and turned on the lights. That's when I realized that it was Eric."

"Was he still conscious? Did he say anything about why he was here?" asked Amanda.

"No." Martin's head sank down on his chest so that his voice was muffled. "Eric was my best friend. I don't know what he was doing here, but whatever it was, I never would have shot him."

The man covered his face with his hands and his shoulders began to shake.

"Stay here with Mr. Chastain," the chief said to his deputy. Then he motioned for Amanda and Nick to go out into the hall with him.

"We found this lying next to the body," the chief said, pulling a plastic evidence bag from his pocket and handed it to us. "It must have fallen out of Devlin's hand when he was shot."

Nick took the bag. He and Amanda stared through the filmy plastic.

"It looks like the locket that Larissa always wore," Amanda said. "She had one around her neck in the coffin."

The chief nodded. "This is the duplicate. The one in the coffin contained pictures of Martin and herself. This one didn't."

"What's in this one?" Nick asked.

The chief put on plastic gloves and opened the bag. He took out the locket. His fingers fumbled with the catch for a moment, but then the locket opened and he held it up. On one side was a picture of Larissa, the same one as was in the other locket, but on the other side was a picture of Eric Devlin.

"No wonder Devlin was trying to get this back," Nick said. "It certainly would prove that he had an intimate relationship with Larissa."

"And give him a motive for killing her," the chief added.

"You mean if she threatened to tell Martin about their affair?" Amanda asked. "But why would she do that? Wouldn't the situation be the same as it was with Kirk—she had more to gain by keeping it quiet?"

"Maybe she fell in love—Eric is more her type than Kirk," Nick said. "What if she wanted to leave Martin for Eric?"

Chief Toth nodded. "That would destroy Eric's business. After all, Martin Chastain was his major client. Maybe he wasn't willing to give up all that for Larissa."

"Eric might have had even more to lose. After all, he and Martin were almost like father and son. It wasn't just the money. He was forced to chose between the two people that he loved," Amanda said.

"From everything I've learned about Larissa, that wouldn't have mattered to her," Nick said. "She had strong emotions. She wanted to have what she wanted to have."

"But does this explain all the other crimes?" asked Amanda.

"I've been thinking about that," the chief said as he returned the locket to its bag. "What if Larissa usually wore the locket with Eric's picture in it when she went to see him? He could have been aware that it existed."

"And Larissa wasn't wearing it the day she was killed because she couldn't find it, according to Mrs. Ames," Amanda said.

"Right. So let's say that Larissa goes to Portland to see Eric in a hotel. Maybe sneaking across the cemetery at night to meet him in his office had gotten too risky, especially once Ben had spotted her. At the hotel she tells Eric that she's going to tell Martin about their affair. He can't talk her out of it, so he decides that he has to kill her. But he doesn't want to kill her in the hotel room because that will lead directly to him."

"So he follows her to her car and kills her on the street in a secluded spot to make it look like a mugging," Nick said.

"But wouldn't they have left the hotel together?" asked Amanda.

The chief frowned. "Maybe not. Possibly he came by himself and booked the room, then she came later to join him. Then they might have left separately as well."

"So he kills her, but he still doesn't have the locket because this was the one time she didn't wear it," Nick said. "That must have worried him."

"Not for long," Amanda said. "Remember, he was at the

funeral when Martin made a big show of putting the locket around Larissa's neck. Probably Eric couldn't believe his good luck when the one piece of evidence that could link him to Larissa disappeared into the coffin where it would probably never be seen again."

"But didn't he know that there were two lockets?" asked Nick.

"I don't think so," Amanda replied. "That's why he tried so hard to retrieve the one from the coffin. He must have been really confused when he broke into the mortuary and found the locket around Larissa's neck didn't have his picture in it. But that confusion must have turned to desperation when Martin mentioned that Larissa had duplicates of most of her stuff. Then he guessed that the locket with his picture in it was still among Larissa's things that Martin was going to go through meticulously."

The chief held up his hand. "Wait a minute. Why do you think that Larissa wouldn't have told Eric about the duplicate locket?"

Amanda smiled. "If she did, Eric would have asked why she had only asked him for one picture. That would have forced her to admit that the other locket contained her husband's picture. If Larissa really loved Eric she probably wouldn't have wanted him to know that."

"So everything is going along fine for Eric until the séance when Larissa's ghost says there might be incriminating evidence in the coffin," said the chief. "That gets Eric to run down to the cemetery that night to break into the mausoleum and try to get the locket. He's interrupted by that kid and bashes him over the head. He's fortunate enough not to be seen, but he still doesn't have what he went for."

"So he goes back for it again on the night that I'm there and hits me on the head," Nick said, considering the idea. "It certainly could have been him that I wrestled with."

"But he still doesn't have the locket," said Amanda, "so he cons the funeral director into leaving his office and breaks in."

"Only to find that the locket around Larissa's neck isn't the one he wants," added the chief. "And then Martin talks about disposing of Larissa's possessions, and he finds out that there's a second locket, the one he's searching for, and that has probably been up in Larissa's bedroom all the time."

"And he has to get it right away because tonight he learns that Martin had already begun going through Larissa's things. Since Martin is supposed to be at the cottage tonight, Eric decides that this is his best chance to retrieve it," Amanda concluded.

Nick shook his head. "You can almost feel sorry for the guy even though he is a killer. For the last few days he must have been going through hell trying to get that locket back."

"And now he ends up dead at the hands of his best friend," the chief said.

"Before we start feeling too sorry for him," Amanda said, "we should remember that he didn't only kill Larissa, he also killed Mrs. Narapov because he thought a second séance would cause more trouble for him."

The chief snapped his fingers. "Wait a minute."

He pulled the evidence bag out of his pocket and held it up to the light of the ornate chandelier. "See there's a gold chain on the locket. That must have been why the medium was having that vision." He cleared his throat deliberately. "Of course, that's only if you believe in that sort of thing."

"She certainly appears to have been on the right track," Amanda said.

"She certainly does," Nick repeated softly.

"What are you going to do next, chief?" Amanda asked.

"Try to confirm all of this speculation by digging up some evidence. I'll start by sending the Portland police pictures of Eric Devlin and Larissa Chastain. They can show them around the hotels downtown and see if anyone remembers their renting a room. If Devlin used his own name or an alias we can identify, we might even be able to find out if he was there on the day of her death."

"Do you think you'll ever have enough evidence that you could have gotten a conviction in court?" asked Amanda.

"Hard to say. But I guess that doesn't really matter now."

They stepped back into the living room. Martin Chastain had sunk back into the sofa and was staring fixedly at the floor.

"First his wife is murdered, then he kills his best friend," said Amanda. "Is there any way to avoid telling him that his wife and best friend were having an affair?"

The chief looked directly into Amanda's eyes. "Don't you think he deserves to know how his wife died? He certainly tried hard enough to find out."

"Yes," she replied. "I suppose you're right."

"But I'm going to wait until I hear from the Portland police about whether there are any witnesses that place Devlin and Mrs. Chastain together that day in Portland," he said more gently. "No sense adding to the old man's pain without any proof."

Chapter Twenty-seven

M arcie sat at the breakfast table feeling angry at being stood up. She had already finished a short stack of blueberry pancakes with a guilt-ridden side order of sausage that she only allowed herself because she had seen someone die last night. And she was feeling more than a little put out at the failure of either Amanda or Nick to make an appearance. It was bad enough that she had been left out of their questioning of Martin Chastain, but now, after they had promised to update her on the investigation in the morning, they were no-shows.

She glanced at her watch. It was 8:30. There was no way early risers like Nick and Amanda were still sleeping, so where were they and why hadn't they bothered to let her know? *Probably off somewhere with that overweight chief of police solving Mrs. Narapov's murder,* she thought, which seemed particularly unfair since she was the only person who had actually been there. It was Saturday, and the restaurant was more crowded than usual, probably with weekend visitors. Marcie had already been on the receiving end of a few pointed glances from the hostess, who clearly wanted to clear her table for those on the waiting line that was starting to form.

Still grumbling to herself, Marcie paid the bill and made a careful note in her little notebook of the amount to be reimbursed by *Roaming New England,* then she made her way into the lobby. She glanced into the sitting room where she and Amanda and Nick had spent so much time discussing the case. She could sit there and wait until they came back from wherever they were. No one could get past her if she carefully watched the hall. But somehow it seemed demeaning to spend all morning waiting for Nick and Amanda. *I have my own car,* she told herself. *There must be somewhere I can go that would be related to the story I'm writing.* Although she hadn't run that morning, Marcie had stepped outside before breakfast and knew that it was a beautiful fall morning, too beautiful to waste sitting around a stuffy lobby waiting for inconsiderate friends.

She went back to her room thinking hard about where she could go. She opened the file on her laptop that contained her story on the Monster of Lake Opal and read it through once again. Maybe that would give her some idea how to spend her morning. Frequently a story that she had considered fully polished the night before would have glaring areas for improvement when read over the next day. But this time, aside from a few minor changes in phrasing, Marcie was very pleased with what she had written. As she imagined the story laid out for the magazine, however, she realized that it would be good to have at least one smashing photo of the lake to put on the first page of the story.

She had lots of photos of the lake from her day spent cruising around with Kirk and Ben. However, the thought occurred to her that the best photo would be one that tied in with the information she had added about Will's childhood friend—maybe a picture taken from the end of the Chastains' dock where Will's friend had left to meet the monster. In her mind's eye, Marcie saw the caption that would say "Photograph of Where Monster was Reportedly Last Sighted." Greg was always saying that in a magazine the extra punch was often in the visual details, and she knew this was just the sort of thing that would please him.

Marcie snatched the car keys off the dresser and pulled on her coat. She could easily drive out to Lake Opal, get the photo, and be back in an hour. After all, she didn't need Amanda's permission to do followup on her own story, she said to herself defiantly. Marcie was smiling happily as she rushed down the stairs and out the front door about two minutes before a still-tired Amanda came down to the dining room.

Marcie drove out to Lake Opal, following the same route she and Amanda had taken the day before, and when she reached the lake she parked in the same lot. She walked down to the shoreline and looked across the lake at the Chastain house, trying to pick out some visual clues that would help her to identify it from the road when she drove around to the other side of the lake. A towering pine tree where the driveway led down to the house seemed to be the most promising landmark. Marcie went back to the car and began her trip around the lake. It took longer than she had expected. Eventually, however, she reached a boat rental dock with a sign that said *South Point Rentals.* There the road made a clear turn and began to head up the other side of the lake.

She continued along, keeping one eye on the road and the other searching the sky for the tall pine. After twenty minutes of driving, which seemed more like half an hour in terms of eyestrain, Marcie was sure that she had somehow managed to miss it. She was ready to turn back, hoping that it would be easier to see from the other side of the road when she went over a small rise. The huge pine suddenly dominated the horizon. She pulled up a few yards past the end of the driveway and stopped the car.

The enthusiasm that had hurried her out of the inn and sustained her in the search for the Chastain house suddenly disappeared, and she sat there uncertain what to do next. Technically speaking she would be trespassing if she walked out on the Chastain dock to take a picture of the lake, although she doubted very much that anyone would mind. In fact, as she stared down the slope through the trees at the dark house, the place looked empty. Nonetheless, she felt a bit like a guilty child who was planning to commit a naughty prank.

Probably I should have run this by Amanda first, she thought. *She would probably have told me to get permission from Martin Chastain first.* Marcie knew that she would have thought of this herself if she hadn't rushed ahead with her idea out of annoyance at being left alone for breakfast. *Well, I can't sit here all morning like a lump,* she told herself. *I should either get the picture, or drive back to the inn and forget the whole thing.*

Marcie thought about what Greg or Amanda would have done under similar circumstances. Greg had been a war correspondent, and occasionally could be cajoled into telling stories about times when he had risked his life to get a good interview. Even Amanda, during her time on the *Boston Globe*, had done things that made summer home trespass seem mild by comparison. Deciding that she was being overly cautious, Marcie pulled the car another ten yards past the driveway and tucked it into a shallow opening in the trees. Somehow it made her feel better not to be too conspicuous about what she was about to do. Pulling the camera out of the bag on the seat next to her, Marcie quietly closed then locked the door.

She walked to the head of the driveway and looked down the slope. A garage was off to the left perpendicular to the driveway, partially hidden by bushes and trees. On the right was the house. The few windows in the front indicated that it had clearly been designed to focus attention on the lake in back, a wide ribbon of blue that filled the horizon. *Probably most of the house's windows were facing in that direction,* Marcie thought, *which will leave me exposed to anyone inside if I walk out on the dock to take a picture.* Deciding that she'd deal with that problem when she came to it, Marcie began to cautiously make her way down the driveway, keeping a careful eye on the house, trying to detect if someone was at home. There was no car in the driveway, but one could be parked in the garage. She decided that when she got to the garage, she'd take a look through the window and see if that was the case.

As she went farther down the driveway and the house came more clearly into view, Marcie guessed that the front door of the house also must face the lake. There was a door and a small porch on the side of the house toward the garage. She was several yards from the garage when she heard the side door open and saw a figure walk out on the porch. Without pausing to think, Marcie dove behind the evergreen bush next to her and squatted down, hoping she wouldn't be seen.

As she watched through the branches, a figure wearing a hooded sweatshirt walked down the driveway and disappeared around the far side of the garage. From his size and the way he walked, Marcie guessed that it was a man, but since the hood covered his head, she couldn't be sure. A moment later he returned, wheeling a black kettle grill, the kind usually used for barbecuing with charcoal. Her father had dragged one around from base to base across the West, but she had never actually seen him use it. She'd asked him once why he kept moving such an awkward thing around when he never barbecued. "It's the sort of thing a man should have," he'd replied with a look that didn't invited further questions.

The hooded man also seemed to have odd ideas about how to barbecue, because he crumbled up a few pages of newspaper that he had brought out of the house with him, then he began filling the kettle with twigs he gathered from around the yard. He went to the side of the porch where some firewood was piled, and using a hatchet, he began to split some larger pieces into kindling. After carefully laying a bed of medium-sized pieces of wood on top of the kindling, he struck a match and set the whole things alight. The wind was blowing in her direction, and Marcie quickly picked up the acrid scent of burning newspaper. The man watched the fire for a minute or so, then he returned to the house.

Marcie's legs began to cramp up and she switched to kneeling on the still hard earth. A chilly breeze was coming off the lake, cutting through her thin jacket. *Why don't I just go up to the guy and introduce myself?* she thought, *instead of hiding in the shrubbery like a crook casing the joint. Maybe I could still do that, just stand up and start walking down the driveway like I was coming around asking permission to take a picture. That would certainly be the sensible thing to do.* But a nagging voice told her to stay where she was, there was something odd going on, and Marcie had a feeling that if she suddenly appeared, the man would stop whatever he was doing. Suddenly she had a driving curiosity to find out what was going to happen next.

She didn't have to wait long. He returned almost immediately with several manila envelopes, which he put on the ground next to the grill. He studied the fire for several more seconds, prodding it a couple of times with a long stick until the flames flared up. When he seemed satisfied, he picked up one of the envelopes and took out some papers and put them on the fire. He watched carefully as the flames shot up, and used the stick to poke the material around in the flames.

Marcie heard a phone ringing in the distance. The man must have heard it too, because he put down the stick and the envelope and headed back to the kitchen. Marcie felt a desire merging on need to find out what the man was burning. There was only one small window next to the door that looked out on the driveway, and although the door had a window that extended halfway down, it appeared to be covered by a sheer curtain. Playing it safe, Marcie went behind the bush and around the back of the garage. She ran across the open space to where the grill was still smoking and stuck her hand into the open envelope on the ground, pulling out a handful of papers. Not daring to look up at the porch for fear that by some form of weird telepathy it would give away her presence, she ran backwards and didn't stop until she was safely back behind the bush.

Marcie sat there for a moment, not looking at what was in her hand, waiting to hear the side door slam open and a man's shouting voice. She figured that she was fast enough to race up the driveway and get into her car before getting caught. But the door didn't open, and after a few minutes, Marcie relaxed. The phone call was clearly taking a while. She decided to glance at what she had taken from the envelope. As she uncurled her hand, she saw that what she had taken included several sheets of paper and a couple of photographs. One picture showed a woman and a man coming out the glass doors of what looked to be an office building or a hotel. The man's face was turned toward the woman so he was only visible in profile, and the woman was smiling happily at whatever he was saying. The second picture was of the same woman, but this time she was alone and standing next to a car. She wasn't smiling this time, but looking behind her apprehensively as if somehow sensing that she was being secretly photographed.

Marcie looked at the sheets of paper. There was a logo at the top that read, "Ace Detective Agency." Underneath were the reassuring words "Discreet, Reliable, and Professional." Marcie could see by the format that it was an investigator's report, but before she could read more, a sound made her turn to look behind her. The hooded man was standing there with the hatchet raised. Marcie had an instant to realize that he must have come out the front door and slipped around the house to get behind her, when the hatchet came forward. She tried to block the blow with her arm, but it had too much force. Something hard hit her head and everything went black.

Chapter Twenty-eight

Amanda waved as Nick stepped into the doorway of the inn's restaurant. Nick said something to the hostess and pointed to Amanda, and the young woman let him walk past the long line of waiting customers.

"Who knew this place got so busy?" Nick said. "I guess it doesn't help that we're having a stylishly late breakfast."

"I was hoping to catch Marcie," Amanda said, glancing at her watch and frowning. "She wasn't in her room. I was hoping that we could check out today. The checkout time is eleven. Maybe she'll be back soon from wherever she went."

"I thought you were going to wait until tomorrow to leave."

"No point in hanging around now that the case is closed. I could use a Sunday at home to do laundry and get ready for work on Monday. Plus I didn't have much of a night's sleep."

"Being up from three until five will do that to you. Were you able to get back to sleep?"

"It took a me over an hour. I think it was close to dawn before I dozed off. What about you?"

"I didn't try."

A harried waitress stopped at the table to drop off Amanda's English muffin. She quickly wrote down Nick's order of scrambled eggs and toast before hurrying away.

"You didn't try to sleep?" Amanda asked with a raised eyebrow.

"Something was bothering me."

"A pea under the mattress?" Amanda asked with a grin.

"Not that kind of bothered." He frowned and rubbed his forehead. Amanda had never seen him look quite so stressed. "I kept thinking about Mrs. Narapov's message. That's what got this whole thing started, you know. Eric would never have tried to retrieve that locket if Mrs. Narapov hadn't gotten Martin all stirred up about exhuming the body. Eric would have figured that the locket was in the coffin with Larissa and would never be seen again."

"I suppose that's true. But what about it?"

"This is going to sound silly, but what bothers me is that Mrs. Narapov's message from Larissa was so close to being right but was still wrong."

Amanda put her coffee cup down, a look of puzzlement on her face.

"Sorry. I'm not following you."

"Look, assume you're like me and don't really believe in this communicating with the next world stuff. The big question then is, how did Mrs. Narapov learn about the locket?"

"Mrs. Ames or anyone else at the funeral could have told her that Martin put it in the casket."

"True. But how would she know that it had anything to do with the identity of the murderer?"

"Somebody who knew about their affair and also knew that Larissa had a locket with Eric's picture in it would have had to tell her," Amanda replied after a moment's thought.

"And who knew about that?" Nick continued, leaning across the table with an urgent expression on his face.

"No one, as far as we know, except for Larissa and Eric."

"And Larissa was dead, and Eric would have no reason to reveal that information."

Amanda nodded. "So you're saying that someone else must have known and told Mrs. Narapov."

"It's even more complicated than that. Someone told the medium to mention that there was a clue in the coffin, which implied that the locket would reveal the murderer's identity. Am I right?"

"Okay."

"But it didn't. The locket had Martin's picture in it. The locket in the coffin wasn't a clue to anything. However, the message was close enough to the truth to play on Eric's worst fears and cause him to become desperate."

"What are you saying? Do you think somebody who knew about the affair and the existence of the locket devised the séance as a way to drive Eric to break into the mausoleum?"

"That was the first step."

"But why would someone do that?"

"Mind if I join you?" Chief Toth asked, pulling out a

chair without waiting for an answer. For a large man he had a way of appearing rather suddenly, Amanda thought, probably a good quality in a police officer.

"How's it going, chief?" Krow said vaguely, still preoccupied with his own line of thought.

"The Portland police have definitely impressed me with their efficiency or else with their excess of manpower. They got a guy over to the hotel nearest to where Larissa was killed. They began checking back to see who rented a room on the day she was killed. Anyone care to guess who's name showed up right away?"

"Eric Devlin?" Amanda asked.

The chief gave her a smile. "Got it in one. The poor fool used his own name, and we know he checked out ten minutes before the approximate time that Larissa was killed. So he could easily have followed her from the hotel, murdered her, then headed back to West Windham. He didn't have an alibi, if you remember."

"Neither did Martin Chastain or Will," Krow said offhandedly.

The chief looked at him sharply.

"Did anyone see Eric around the inn last night?" Nick asked.

"Not that we've found. Nobody saw any of our suspects, but lots of businesses haven't opened for the day yet. I still have hopes."

Krow shrugged as if it didn't matter.

"Do you have something on your mind that I should hear about?" the chief asked.

"Nick is bothered by the fact that Mrs. Narapov's message was just close enough to the truth to get Eric started on his search for the locket," Amanda said, then she sketched out Nick's theory.

The chief held up a hand. "Wait a minute. Are you saying that someone knew Eric had killed Larissa and was trying to set him up to incriminate himself by breaking into the mausoleum?"

"More than that," said Nick. "It wasn't enough to frighten Eric into breaking into the mausoleum, he also had to lure him into breaking into the Chastain house looking for the other locket so he could be killed."

The chief shook his head and gave Amanda a small smile as if pleading for support in the face of such insanity. "Sounds awfully complicated to me, Krow."

"We're not dealing with a normal mind here, Chief. The person who planned this out was very intelligent but also pretty twisted. He wanted to make Eric suffer as much as he had by making him jump through hoops, then end Eric's life in a way that would tarnish his reputation."

"All pretty dramatic," the chief muttered. "Any candidates?"

"There's only one possibility," said Nick. "It had to be someone who knew about the affair between Eric and Larissa and who knew about the locket with Eric's picture in it."

"But we have no idea who, if anyone, knew all that."

"And," Nick continued, "it had to be the person who employed Mrs. Narapov."

Marcie woke up with a raging headache and a throat so dry she wasn't able to swallow. It took her a moment to realize that there was a gag shoved into her mouth. She pushed it forward with her tongue. That helped a little, but it was tied into her mouth and with her hands bound behind her back there wasn't much more she could do. Her feet were also tied tightly together. The only good thing about the situation was that she hadn't been locked in a closet. She was on the floor of what appeared to be a bedroom.

By leaning back against the bed and pushing with her feet, she managed to lever herself up until she was sitting on the bed. She was about to hop across the room and try to reach the door when it swung open and the hooded figure came into the room. He pushed back the hood, and Marcie was surprised to see that it was an older man. His white hair stood on end in back from the rubbing of the hood, giving him an indecisive, quizzical look. But there was nothing unsure about the way he walked quickly across the room and pulled her to her feet.

"Hop," he ordered, holding firmly to her arm and forcing her forward.

By the time she reached the living room, she was glad to flop back on the sofa. Hopping with your feet tied together wasn't all that easy, and she would have fallen a couple of times if he hadn't held her upright.

"I'm kind of sorry to see that you're awake. I was planning to carry you outside, then run you down to the end of the dock in the wheelbarrow. From there it would be easy to dump you into the boat. But at least now I won't have to carry you. I can have you hop out onto the porch after you've rested a minute and put you in the wheelbarrow out there."

The man said all this in a straightforward way like he was telling her about some kind of new landscaping plan that he had in mind. Marcie went cold. She would have felt better if he had ranted and raved like a madman. The matter-of-factness in his tone made the whole thing seem sensible and at the same time unstoppable.

"You hit me on the head," she said, trying to work up some anger to offset her fear.

"You're lucky I used the blunt end of the hatchet. Of course, I only did that to avoid getting blood on the ground. That would be hard to conceal."

"Why are we going out in the boat?" Marcie asked, knowing that sounded dumb but at a loss for words.

"I've filled a sturdy, plastic garbage bag with heavy rocks. When we get on the boat, I'll tie the bag firmly to the rope around your legs. Once we're in the middle of the lake, I'll shove you over the side. It's a very deep lake, so if I'm reasonably lucky no one will ever discover your body. I've found your car. I'll take that back into town after I'm done here and park it somewhere with the keys inside. Maybe I'll be lucky twice and a rustic hoodlum will steal it."

Marcie felt a scream rising in the back of her throat and fought to keep it down.

"Who are you?" she asked.

"I might ask you the same thing, since this is my house," the man said, taking out a small comb and running it through his hair. It made him look less crazy, but Marcie didn't think it had any impact on the inner man.

"You're Martin Chastain?"

The man nodded.

Marcie cleared her throat and tried to sound calm. "I'm Marcie Ducasse. I work for *Roaming New England* magazine; I think there's been some misunderstanding. I just stopped by to get a picture of the lake from your dock. I'm writing an article about the Monster of Lake Opal, and I wanted a photo to go with it."

"And how does going through my private papers fit in with your article?"

Marcie paused, knowing she was on weak ground. She gave a trembling smile. "I guess I just got curious. I saw you burning the stuff and wondered what it was."

"Well, that was a mistake. I'd have been happy to let you take a picture of the lake if you'd just come to the door and asked. But now you've gotten involved in my business."

"All I saw were a couple of pictures of a woman and a man. They're strangers to me. I don't know anything about what's going on here." Marcie heard her voice getting a little shrill. She took a deep breath and told herself that getting excited wasn't going to help the situation.

"Maybe it doesn't mean anything to you right now. But once you talked to your friends, Krow and Vickers, you'd piece it all together. And you saw the letterhead that said that it was a report from a private investigator. The chief would find out soon enough from them that I knew all about Larissa's various affairs because I've had her followed from the beginning of our marriage."

"So you knew about . . ."

"The golf pro and Kirk Ames. Of course, but none of that bothered me."

"It didn't?" Marcie said, surprise driving out fear for a moment.

"I knew when I married her that she wouldn't be faithful. She wasn't that kind of woman. What exciting woman would be faithful to a man over thirty years older than herself? But when she took up with Eric—" the man stopped.

His face contorted in pain and for a moment he couldn't go on. "He was like a son, and she got him to betray me. That was more than I could take—from either of them."

Marcie's mind raced as she tried to think of another question to ask, anything to delay hopping across the room and out into the wheelbarrow like so much garden mulch. Once in the wheelbarrow she had a feeling there would be nothing that she could do to stop her inevitable journey to the cold bottom of Lake Opal. *Maybe I'll at least get to see the monster,* she thought, and felt hysterical laughter forcing its way up her throat. She swallowed hard.

"What about Mrs. Narapov?"

"Foolish woman. I paid her well to put on that phony séance. I told her word for word what to say. I knew it would turn Eric's life into hell once he thought that we were going to find the locket. He didn't know that I had hidden both of them of the day I planned to kill Larissa. Later I made of point of dramatically putting the one with Larissa and myself in the coffin without revealing which one it was. I even concocted the absurd story about Larissa's fear of being buried alive, so he knew the coffin would be accessible. All of it was aimed at moving Eric down the path that led to my bedroom last night. You should have seen the surprised look on his face when I walked into the room and shot him twice in cold blood."

"You had this whole séance thing planned from the start?"

"From before I struck my beautiful, unfaithful wife over the head."

"And then you murdered Eric."

"Punished him for betraying me. What kind of a son

sleeps with his father's wife?" Chastain smiled. "Has rather the ring of a Greek tragedy, don't you think?"

"But why did you kill Mrs. Narapov?"

"When I asked her to do another phony séance to prolong Eric's anguish, she got nervous and refused. Then she tried to blackmail me. She suspected that something funny was going on and said she'd go to the chief and tell him that I'd told her what to say unless I paid her off. I didn't trust her to keep quiet even if I gave her money so I had to kill her, although it wasn't part of the original plan."

He got to his feet and walked across the room toward Marcie. He grabbed her by the arm and easily pulled her to her feet. She was surprised at his strength.

"Now hop toward the kitchen," he ordered, holding firmly to her arm.

Marcie took three hops then jerked herself sideways hard, breaking his grip and falling to the floor. She couldn't get away, but she wasn't going to make it easy for him to carry out his plan. When she rolled onto her back and looked up, she saw that a gun had appeared in his hand.

"Do that again," he said calmly, "and I will shoot you and dump your body in the lake. I would rather not have to clean up the cabin, but if I'm careful it won't make much of a mess. And in case you think that I won't do it because someone will hear the shot, rest assured that there is no one else around this time of year so I am not in the least concerned. Do we understand each other?"

Marcie allowed herself to be dragged back to her feet.

Chapter Twenty-nine

"This all sounds pretty crazy to me," Kirk Ames said from the back seat of the patrol car, where he was sitting next to Amanda.

The chief, Krow, and Amanda had gone to Martin Chastain's house and been informed by Mrs. Ames that he was currently staying at the cottage by the lake. Kirk had been there visiting his mother, and the chief had decided that having a deputy along would be a good idea and had ended his officer's suspension on the spot.

"It sort of makes sense of all the facts," the chief said, watching the twisting road as he went well above the speed limit.

"Why didn't he kill me then? I had an affair with his wife," the young man asked in a soft voice.

"Probably because you weren't his best friend," Amanda answered.

The chief took the shortest way to the cottage, so he went around the lake the opposite way that Marcie had gone. He slowed as he came to the car parked a few yards from the driveway.

"That's Marcie's car," Amanda said.

"Chastain might be holding her," Krow added.

The chief picked up his microphone and called in for the two deputies on patrol to come to the Chastain house.

"We can't wait here for backup," Amanda said. "He could be killing her right now."

The chief nodded, and everyone got out of the car.

"Kirk, you come with me. The rest of you wait here."

"I don't have a weapon," Kirk said.

Toth popped the trunk and handed him the shotgun.

"I think we should all go down there," Krow said, staring down the driveway. "Chastain is at least a little crazy, and he might listen to one of us more than to you."

The chief hesitated for a moment. "Okay," he finally said, drawing his weapon, "but you two stay behind us."

He set off at a quick pace down the driveway with Kirk on his left holding the shotgun out in front of him.

"Do you have any idea how Marcie ended up out here?" Nick asked.

Amanda shook her head in reply.

When they were parallel with the side door, the chief started to go up on the porch, but Kirk, who had gone a little further past the house, stopped him.

"I see a man walking out on the dock."

The chief bounded off the porch faster than Amanda would have thought possible, and he and Kirk ran around to the front of the house. The four of them stood there for a moment, watching a man push a wheelbarrow out to the end of the dock.

"I see an arm hanging over the side!" Krow shouted.

With Kirk and the Toth leading the way, the four of them charged onto the long dock that extended out into the lake. They had only gone halfway out when the vibrations must have given them away. Martin Chastain turned to them and pointed the gun down at the figure in the barrel.

"I'll shoot her if you come any closer."

"And we'll shoot you!" Kirk shouted, walking forward with the shotgun braced against his shoulder.

"That won't make her any less dead."

"Hold it!" the chief ordered. Kirk stopped but his body still leaned forward eager to make a move.

"That's sensible. Now drop your guns on the dock," Chastain said.

The chief bent down and carefully placed his gun right in front of him on the boards. Kirk reluctantly did the same with the shotgun.

"Kick them into the water."

Amanda saw Chief Toth frown for a moment as if trying to solve a knotty problem. Finally he shook his head.

"I'm not going to do that. You kill that girl if you have to, but I'm not going to put you in a position to kill all four of us."

It was Chastain's turn to pause. He suddenly turned his back to them. With one swift motion he spun the wheelbarrow and dumped Marcie off the dock into the water. Then he turned and ran for the boat.

Not even bothering to reach down and pick up the shotgun, Kirk sprinted toward the end of the dock. The chief paused to retrieve his automatic, then he began moving at a slow trot with Amanda and Nick right behind. Amanda thought that Kirk was trying to catch Chastain, but without pausing he dove into the water right where Chastain had dumped Marcie. The roar of an outboard motor filled the air, and by the time his pursuers had pushed the wheelbarrow out of the way and reached the end of the dock, Martin Chastain was heading out into the lake.

Chief Toth stood for an instant with the gun clenched in his hand as if trying to decide whether to take a shot, then he relaxed.

"Damn fool can't go anywhere. What's he going to do when he gets to land? Walk to the road and hitch a ride?" He took the cell phone off his belt. I'll call the state police and see if they can get a couple of cars around to help us. My other deputies will be here in a couple of minutes, they can be around to the other side of the lake pretty much by the time Chastain gets there." He punched in some numbers, not taking his eyes off the boat.

Amanda rushed to the side of the dock where Marcie had gone in and saw that she was managing to stay afloat by doing some of kind of awkward seal-like motion. Kirk had just reached her side. He turned her over and putting one arm across her chest, he stroked with the other and began to guide her to a ladder that led up to the top of the dock. Nick stood at the top of the ladder ready to help them up.

Amanda turned and saw that the chief was still staring across the lake as if by sheer force of will he could reverse the boat's direction. The man behind the wheel was so far away that he was nothing more than a dark blur when it happened. A long, curving object suddenly rose out of the water. The bow hit it and the boat sailed high in the air, performing a graceful somersault, before crashing back hard onto the water. Then an echoing silence as the motor sputtered and died. Slowly what appeared to be an arched neck with a small head on top submerged.

"Well," the chief said after a long moment, looking at the phone in his hand as if wondering how it had come to be there. "I guess he hit one of those submerged logs."

The chief gave Amanda a long look.

"That's what it's going to be in my report. Pretty hard to say any different from this distance, wouldn't you agree?"

Amanda said nothing.

Chapter Thirty

"Are you sure you don't want to wait until tomorrow to leave?" Amanda asked. "We could spend another night here?"

They were sitting in the front room of the inn. It was Saturday afternoon. After the morning's events at Lake Opal, they'd gone to the hospital to have Marcie examined. She'd finally been given a clean bill of health, along with a firm warning that she should report to the nearest hospital at the first sign of a concussion. Then they'd gone to the police to provide witness statements concerning the death of Martin Chastain. A dive team was already out looking for his body.

Marcie shook her head. "Nope. I've really had it with this place. I think I'd prefer to get back to Wells and spend the night in my own bed."

"There seemed to be one thing that you liked about the town."

"What's that?" Marcie asked, then she got Amanda's point and grinned.

She and Kirk had spent a long time talking outside the hospital. Marcie wasn't quite sure, but she thought that she had pretty much forgiven him for being a jerk. Forgiven him enough at least to give him a second chance.

"Well, he did save my life."

"I thought you were doing a pretty good job of staying afloat before he got to you."

"Yeah, but I couldn't have climbed those stairs with my feet tied together," Marcie said, grinning. "He wasn't completely useless."

"Plus, he is cute."

"Oh, yeah."

"And he doesn't live *that* far away."

"Just far enough so if we break up, I won't run into him at the grocery store," she said, repeating Amanda's earlier comment.

Amanda laughed. "There is that."

Marcie paused and a speculative look passed over her face. "For my story on the Monster of Lake Opal, do you think I could mention that you . . ."

"No," Amanda said firmly.

"But you were the only one of us who saw it. I didn't see anything. Neither did Kirk. Nick is really ticked that he was helping me up the ladder when the boat crashed. Of course I'm not sure whether he's mad because he didn't see the monster or because he can't conclusively say that you're wrong. Only you and the chief saw anything, and the chief insists it was just a giant log that got shoved out of the water."

"Yeah, a giant log with a curved neck and a little head on top," Amanda said. "You see one of those every day."

"You were pretty far away. And in your witness statement, didn't you say that it could possibly have been some kind of sea animal?"

"I didn't want to make trouble for the chief. But I know what I saw."

It had been bad enough having this discussion with Nick down at the police station. Having gullible Marcie being the voice of reason was too much. Amanda gave her an intimidating glance.

"Well then, if you're so sure about what you saw," Marcie said, "don't our readers deserve to know?"

Amanda shook her head. "Never put yourself in the story. If we had another witness who would confirm it, that would be fine. But I'm not going to be the only one who says she saw a monster out there. Anyway, we can't put anything about the Chastain case in the article because it hasn't been completely sorted out yet. Go with what you had before. You can always write a follow-up piece later. We'll buy Ben a new camera, maybe he'll come up with a great digital shot of the monster some day."

"Yeah, he deserves a present for all his help." Marcie stood. "Well, I'm going upstairs to finish my packing. Are you coming?"

"I'm going to wait here for Nick. He said he was leaving right away."

"Tell him good-bye for me, will you?"

"You can tell him yourself. Here he is."

Marcie met Nick in the hallway. After talking for a moment, they hugged. Marcie headed up the stairs, and Nick came into the room to join Amanda. He sat on the old horse-hair sofa and crossed one leg over the other, looking as relaxed as always.

"So you were right about Mrs. Narpov's message being a hoax," Amanda said. "It was all part of Martin's plan to kill Eric."

"But I never figured that he'd killed Larissa," Nick said. "I guess finding out about his wife and his surrogate son was too much for him."

"Being betrayed by either one of them, he might have handled, but being betrayed by both at the same time was too much. What I can't believe is how he planned the whole thing out like a play with him in the leading role. His shattered-old-man act really had me fooled."

"Will told me that his father had done some acting in college. I just never put it all together."

"He was a brilliant man. His genius showed in everything he did, for better or worse."

Krow shook his head sadly, then mustered a smile. "I told you that it would be fun to attend a séance. Plus you got to see the Monster of Lake Opal."

"Don't start," Amanda warned. "And as odd as it sounds, it was fun."

"So would you do it again another time?"

"You mean go to a séance?" she asked.

"I was thinking more specifically about whether you'd come up this way to visit me. I can't promise multiple murders and monsters every time, but I'll do my best to make it stimulating."

Amanda glanced at her watch. It was just 4:00. Tomorrow morning Jeff would be getting behind the wheel of his packed car, hoping that the phone would ring at the last minute. It would be wrong to make him wait any longer. She took out her cell phone, finally feeling able to make the call.

Krow raised a quizzical eyebrow but said nothing.

She'd feel bad disappointing Jeff, but knew she'd feel worse if she disappointed herself. Right now she needed the excitement of this job, and the friends she shared it with.

Amanda smiled at Nick. "Make your invitation interesting enough, and I'll be back."